UPSTREAM

By Donald McEwing

Dedicated to Virginia

Flectere si nequeo superos acheronta movebo

Virgil, *Aeneid,* Book VII

Table of Contents

These notes and stories come from the estate of my great uncle, Professor George Angle. He taught at a Northeastern university, and his expertise with ancient languages, rare texts, and mysterious inscriptions attracted scholars from around the world seeking his knowledge and insight. He wrote extensively about the history of the Necronomicon, *its suppression, and the cult of the talisman. Professor Angle lived in Providence and passed away in Newport, Rhode Island on November 23, 1932 at the age of 82. As sole heir and executor, I have tried to honor his memory by arranging these notes and stories into a coherent whole and make sense of them, despite their strange content.*

– Francis Thermonde

Northwestern Greenland

501 A.D.

The source of the call comes from upstream. The goal of my spiritual quest awaits.

It comes to me in a dream. In the beginning, it is as weak as a newborn calf, but like a young caribou, it quickly grows stronger. Now it draws me. A glacier offers a convenient path towards my goal, so I follow this broad frozen river and I hike north, upstream.

I am White Shade, Shaman of the people. According to tradition, a dream of power comes once in a lifetime. This is my dream of power, and so I must leave my wives and children and the comfort of the village, and pursue the dream alone, in perpetual daylight, beneath the overarching dome of the blue sky. Perpetual daylight can cause snow blindness; as much as I dislike them, I wear my snow goggles. The narrow slits in the bone protect my eyes but restrict my vision. It is a long, slow, dangerous ascent up the glacier. The danger of falling through its pitted glacial ice worries me. To avoid hidden snow bridges and chasms, I must probe the surface with a narwhale tusk before each step. Also, there is the risk of injury. Even a sprained ankle would be disastrous. Polar bears are always a hazard, although it would be unusual to see one this far inland. The cost of this quest could be my life, but I rest easy knowing my apprentice, Wise Woman, will take my place should the quest fail; still, the people cannot afford to lose another male. I must succeed.

After hiking north for days, the terrain changes. The glacial river becomes a plateau stretching for as far as the eye can see. The ice on the plateau looks different, too. It is hard, smooth, and flat; strangest of all, it is completely clear. It is like walking atop the dome of the sky and looking down.

The call strengthens. I am almost out of food. Only a handful of caribou strips remain.

At last, I reach the place of astonishing power. I stand on the edge of a precipice where the crevasse dives deep into the clear ice. The call comes from the depths, and strange noises accompany the call, strange mad whistling music. It threatens yet compels. I cannot concentrate. My head feels like it is being turned inside out. I lose all track of time as I stand with my arms at my side, motionless. My apprentice would laugh and call my confusion 'the astonishment disease.'

My goal pulls me towards the depths. I am tempted to throw myself headlong into the chasm. Is this what the call wants, or is it my way of resisting it? Is it a song luring me to destruction, or preservation? My apprentice used to make fun of me for being afraid of dying, but she is not here, and this is not the same, for death might be better than what awaits in the crevasse. At last, I decide. I take off my snow goggles, strap on my leather and bone crampons, and using my sturdiest knives as pitons I descend the sheer walls. I drive in the pitons with my ice axe, descend, and remove them again. It is slow going, and I dare not look down. This place is disorienting. The clear ice captures the sunlight, so I can see very well even though I am far below the surface.

The snow here does not behave properly. It falls upward, from the depths to the chasm's rim.

The mad whistling noise peaks in intensity, and then changes into a nonsensical, repetitive sound:

Mayday, Mayday...

The voice is male, but not one that I recognize, and if the sounds are words, they are not like any words spoken by the people. It seems to come from far away, yet it echoes from wall to wall.

And then I see it, deep within the clear ice: the object of my spiritual quest.

Within is a black, unmoving body. It appears to be dead. How could anything survive being trapped in the ice? It looks larger than a person or a bear, but it is not a person, or bear, or caribou, or seal. It has a black shell, five thick arms like a sea star, and five ridges running along its body. The top has no eyes or ears or mouth, just nodes encircling the head, if it has one.

It does not belong in this world.

How long has it been there? Since it is deep inside the clear ice, it must have been there a very long time. I call it an Old One.

The man's nonsense words stop, but the mad whistling continues during my ascent. The climb is difficult, but I am so amazed by what I have seen that I hardly notice. Finally, the peculiar whistling stops when I reach the rim. Once there, I pull my best tooth from my pack, a large whale tooth. I use my best knife and chant while I carve a likeness of the Old One. It takes a long time. My chant imbues it with magic, for I am the Shaman of my people and I am fulfilling my quest. I have created an idol, a talisman pulsing with power.

It is a long walk back to the village. Despite the perpetual daylight it is unusually cold, but my furs provide excellent insulation. I have a bigger problem. I took too much time hiking north and then carving the talisman, and now I am hiking south and out of food. There are no animals to hunt. Hunger and the cold take their toll and I grow weaker.

The people are not far but I can go no further. This is the end. The talisman compels me to one last act. I disrobe and hold the talisman high over my head. Now I wait for the cold to finish me off. If the people find my body... when... I will be posed with the talisman held in outstretched arms over my head. They will know what to do.

Baghdad

September 1, 901 A.D.

The Tigris flows not far from the House of Wisdom, and although I cannot see or hear it, I sense the river's heavy presence. The afternoon racket of the round city of Baghdad floats through the labyrinthine streets to the second story window and into my small study room- children shouting, women chatting by the riverside, men hawking goods in a nearby bazaar- and in the distance, a blind muezzin calls the faithful to prayer from a high minaret. No one is around, so I can safely ignore the call, leave the prayer rug rolled in the corner, and focus on translating the ancient papyrus text.

A breath of wind comes through the window. In its own way, the air flow is a wonder. Thanks to those clever Persians, the House of Wisdom architecture creates its own breezes by taking advantage of the interior courtyard's shade and air currents, thereby making the House habitable even in summer heat. Yet this breath of wind cannot be the result of architectural design. The wind is far too cold. Such a wind should not be possible on the first day of September.

A sickly yellow overcast lingers from the latest dust storm. Not even closing the windows and doors can prevent the sand from getting into every nook and crevice. And for all their cleverness, the Persians cannot do much about the smells of the city.

A knock on the door interrupts my musings. "Who's there?"

"Abdul?" It is a deep familiar voice. "Abdul Alhazred? Are you in there?"

"Of course."

"May I come in?"

Ah! How can I translate without the silence so necessary for thought? With a sigh I a lean forward in my simple wooden chair, and, using an ink-stained thumb and index finger, I extinguish the candle. Even this ordinary act gives me pause. For a translator, everything becomes fraught with symbolic intent. It is an occupational hazard, I suppose; here is an example: according to the Persians, the people to their East, the Indians and Chinese, believe each finger represents one of the five essential elements. The index finger stands for fire. The others represent air, earth, and water, and the thumb stands for the fifth, invisible, quintessential element; furthermore, each conveys symbolic content through gesture. By putting out the candle's flame with my thumb and forefinger, I am applying the fifth element- the quintessence- to the element of fire, and so I put out a small yellow flame. The room feels noticeably colder when I pinch the wick. A thin, sickly gray wisp of smoke rises from it like a miniature plume from some nameless volcanic mountain. It matters not; I place the quill in its well and push parchments, papers, and books to one side of the desk. Dust motes from the musty volumes swirl into the air.

I cross the blue tile floor and open the door. "Enter."

My visitor- a fit man of medium height, with a black beard and lively eyes- comes in with a bounce in his step, and smiles. His teeth are even and white. He wears a traditional silk robe and leather sandals, both expensive by the looks of them. Ah, the cost. I know nothing about such things. He offers a traditional greeting.

"And peace unto you," I respond, accompanied by a cursory touch of the hand to the forehead and the slightest bow. With that, I laugh, and put my hand on his big shoulder. "Abu, you are back! How I have missed you."

Abu Zayd al-Balkhi, from the city of Herat, is the greatest living scientist in the Caliphate, as well as explorer, geographer, and psychologist. He pulls up a chair and we sit facing one another at the desk. Arching one eyebrow, he produces a ripe pomegranate from his robe and places it on his desk. He knows how much I like them. "Yes, I have returned."

"How long has it been?" I ask.

"Three years. And how are you, old friend?"

"I am not that old." In fact, we are the same age, 41.

He lowers his voice to a conspiratorial whisper. "You sure act old. The students say you are mad."

"Not mad enough to sail off the edge of the world," I scoffed. It was a shared joke. Thanks to the Palace of Wisdom astronomers and mathematicians, we both know perfectly well that the earth is a sphere with a circumference of about 24,000 miles.

Al-Balkhi glances back at the window and gathers his robe about him. "It's cold." He returns his attention to the table and touches a paper. "Still translating pagans, I see."

"The Prophet instructs us to pursue knowledge to the ends of the earth-"

"-Even to China."

"Even to China," I echo, completing the quotation from the Koran. It is an instruction taken quite literally. Scholars from around the world are heeding the call of the Prophet. They are bringing manuscripts and ancient texts to Baghdad, the cultural capital of the world, for translation into Arabic. Scholars from the House of Wisdom are also striking out seeking manuscripts and texts. "So, you went to China," I mutter without thinking.

An awkward silence follows. His most recent trip is supposed to be a state secret, commissioned by the current Abbasid Caliph, al-Mutadid Billah. He has held power for the past nine years, and he is the one covering the cost- ah, the cost- of my studies in the House of Wisdom. In the ambitious tradition of previous Caliphs, he is transforming the city into the intellectual center of the world and memorializing it with stunning architectural design. He is also known for cruelty, torture, and bloody military conquests. Obviously, it is a good idea to avoid discussing anything untoward.

I wipe my bluish-black stained fingers on my cheap cotton robe. "This new lampblack is impossible to wash off."

"Oil and soot can be difficult," he observes. Another awkward silence follows.

"Listen-"

"It's all right, my friend." He reaches across and pats my arm. "Relax. I have already reported to the Caliph, and he sent me directly to you."

My jaw drops. The Caliph knows of me?

He idly fingers a parchment on my desk. "What are you translating?"

"The works of a Roman, Virgil."

"May I?" He peruses it. Not only is al-Balkhi a great explorer, he possesses an extraordinary mind, even by the standards of the top scholars in this Golden Age of Islam. He speaks several languages and is conversant in fields as diverse as the pagan's ancient "rational science," new technologies, philosophy, and optics. He reads a line aloud:

Flectere si nequeo superos acheronta movebo.

"Translation?" I ask.

He strokes his black beard. "Latin, of course. Did Virgil steal this from the ancient Greeks?" He pauses and gives me an exaggerated wink. "Or does it have something to do with a sunken city?"

"It originated with Virgil, as far as I know, and has nothing to do with Atlantis." He knows I am passionate about anything to do with the mythical sunken city, originally described by the great pagan Plato in a dialogue. "So, tell me, how would you translate it?"

"If I cannot bend the heavens above, I will move hell." He clears his throat. "By 'the heavens above' he means paradise, of course."

"Of course." His translation is good, and I nod in appreciation. "Allow me to offer an alternative: 'If I cannot bend the heavens above, I will cross the Acheron'."

He purses his lips. "The quote contrasts opposites- heaven and hell."

"The passage specifically mentions the Acheron."

"So?"

"In pagan mythology, the Acheron- the river of woe- surrounds hell. It flows backwards. The dead cross it on a ferry; however, those who are neutral in life do not take the ferry. They do not stand, or fight, or live, or die. They merely sit on the riverbank, unable to commit."

The explorer closes his eyes and nods, and then fixes me with a stare. "You mean, like you?"

I lift my chin, sit up straight, and throw my shoulders back. "I am committed to knowledge," I dramatically declare.

"Committed to sitting is more like it." We both laugh. "Seriously, my friend, be careful. There are those who value belief over knowledge. They see challenges as heresy, including everything to do with the House of Wisdom."

"How can new fields of mathematics be heretical? Algebra-"

"-Did you now it means 'the reunion of broken parts'? he interrupts. "I always like that."

"-Spherical trigonometry-"

"Look, you know how I feel-"

"-Non-Euclidean geometry-" I continue, talking over him.

"I am trying to be helpful."

"Belief and practice should be driven by reason, not claims of infallibility based on a book."

"Be careful, Abdul."

I cannot resist taking a sarcastic tone. "Am I turning my back on paradise because of my commitment to knowledge? Am I crossing a ferry into hell?"

"Stop. That's enough."

I take a deep breath, survey my small study, and sigh. "This House of Wisdom is just a glorified library."

Al-Balkhi gives me a sympathetic smile. "Many believe glory belongs to mosques, not libraries."

"Oh, come on. No one takes me seriously. I am just an academic. The students call me 'The Mad Arab'."

"They say you found something in the ruins of Babylon."

"Not true."

"They say you are an alchemist and have recreated a magical metal that once formed the inner ring wall of Atlantis. What is it called again?" He strokes his beard and tries to recall the name for it. "It glows... fiery red-"

"-Orichalcum."

"Yes, that's it! And they say you spent years wandering the Empty Quarter- the Crimson Desert- and met an invisible monster who promised to devour you in broad daylight." He struggles to keep a straight face, but cannot, and we both laugh.

"Listen," I say, "I was born in Sana'a, a city so lovely they call it 'Happy Arabia' because everyone talks in verse." Abu snorts good-naturedly in disbelief. "And then," I continue, "I lived in Damascus, the City of Jasmine, just to smell the perfume of its soft white flowers in the spring."

He rolls his eyes. "You people from Yemen are all the same, a bunch of eccentric poets. When are you going to stop translating and write something original?"

"Funny you should mention that. Last night I dreamed I wrote a book. It contained all the knowledge from the House of Wisdom."

"Forget dreams," he says with the wave of a hand. "Here." He reaches into a pocket of his silk robe and produces a piece of soft off-white cloth wrapped around an object which he places it on the desk in front of me. He gazes at me with peculiar intensity. "Write about this."

Something about it makes me recoil. "What is it?"

He pushes it towards me. "Open it."

Inside I find a small curiously disturbing carved ivory object. Just looking at it hurts my eyes. "Where did you get this? China?"

He shakes his head. "In accordance with the Caliph's order and the Prophet's instruction, I sailed as far north as possible, seeking knowledge."

"This looks like an idol, or talisman." I leave the hideous object in the middle of the table. I cannot bring myself to touch it.

"Perhaps. An idol is to be worshipped. If that is the case, we should destroy it immediately, since idolatry is forbidden."

"Of course."

"Then again, a talisman is not an object of worship. It holds magical power."

"So, we will regard this object as a talisman."

"Just so."

"What is it?" It is common for people to wear amulets to harness supernatural power, usually in the form of a stone in a chord around the neck. Islam approves of this pagan practice; nevertheless, I examine the object without touching it. The ivory white carving looks like a cross between a sea star, beetle, and cactus. Five thick starfish-shaped appendages form its base. The body resembles a barrel, and a set of nodes encircles the top.

"It resembles nothing I have ever seen. The Caliph wishes you to bring your knowledge of other cultures and mythologies to this, and write a thorough analysis answering a basic question: 'What is it'?"

I quail at the prospect of writing about this monstrous thing, yet it draws me like a magnet. Even speaking in its presence is difficult.

"How... Where...?"

"Would you like to hear how I obtained it?"

"Yes." I can barely manage the strangled assent.

"I traveled north as far as possible, seeking new knowledge."

"North," I echo.

"I commissioned the construction of a sturdy sea-going vessel in Damascus and named the craft *The Reunion of Broken Parts*. It featured a double hull with a thin layer of copper between the layers of wood, as well as a thicker one reinforcing the prow. I hired a crew of 22 brave Syrian sailors and a helmsman experienced with the world beyond The Passage-"

"- The Straits."

"Correct. The helmsman's name was D'Anforth. Together we sailed to the Emirate of Sicily under the banner- the black flag of the Abbasid Caliphate- to do our part for this Golden Age of Islam."

"God is great," I say.

"Indeed. After loading additional provisions in Palermo, including a quantity of Greek Fire, we proceeded along the coast of Andalusia, through The Passage, and north to the Emirate of Córdoba."

"The cost must have been astronomical," I observe. *Ah, the cost.*

"No doubt. In the great port of Lisbon, they informed us that hugging the coast would take us past hostile Christian kingdoms, and then to the lands of the pagan Rus, a tall, warlike, blonde and red-haired people. The Rus cover themselves in tattoos from head to foot. They are a handsome people, and yet their hygiene is disgusting."

I hold up a hand in a warding gesture. "I don't want to know."

He ignores me. "Some of their habits are truly strange. Did you know they comb their hair every single day?"

"How odd."

"Indeed! Beyond the Rus live impoverished nomadic tribes, the Sami. They survive in the frozen northern wastes by herding reindeer."

"What manner of animal is that?"

"It's like a giant deer," he explains. "In any case, the Córdobans were very helpful. I gathered as much information as possible and reported it to the Caliph upon my return. There seemed little point in sailing northeast beyond the Rus and Sami. Those tribes are already known to us. I sought new knowledge."

"Go on. What about this talisman?" The ivory figurine is already insinuating its strangeness into my head.

"According to the Córdobans, due north lay lands of little value, inhabited by farmers, cloistered Christians, and armored warriors in perpetual battle with raiders- Rus Vikings- and, even farther north, by hairy pagan brutes who paint themselves blue and worship trees. Like the Rus and Sami, these people are already known to the Caliphate and offer little in the way of new knowledge. And so, keeping well away from the coast in order to avoid the warlike Christians of the Kingdom of León, we sailed north by northwest. We voyaged into the fastness of an open, unknown ocean." He pauses and stares into the distance, and whispers "empty and deserted the sea."

"The talisman- tell me!"

He holds up a hand, refusing to be rushed. "We sailed 2,000 miles before making landfall. A gigantic wave appeared out of nowhere and nearly swamped *The Reunion of Broken Parts*, but we survived and continued northwards another 500 miles along a cold, barren, rocky coast. Expeditions inland revealed an endless sheet of ice. As we sailed, we encountered various tribes. The Rus called them Skraelings- barbarians- because they were primitive even by Rus standards. The northernmost tribes called themselves the Inuit. They wore furs made from animals such as caribou-"

"- Caribou?"

"Another kind of giant deer, but unlike the reindeer, these cannot be tamed. The Skraelings lived inside domes made from blocks of ice, and they used harpoons to hunt. They survived by eating birds, fish, and seals. And there were fierce enormous bears, white bears-"

"Yes, yes, now what about the talisman?"

He gives me a long stare, and nods to himself. "We proceeded north until ice stopped our progress. At that northernmost point we encountered a degenerate tribe, an offshoot of the Inuit, and there I acquired the talisman." He flashes a crooked smile. "Go ahead. Pick it up."

My curiosity overcomes my reluctance and I do so. It weighs more than expected, and its appearance is wrong, all wrong, a monstrous and impossible creation. Touching the figurine causes a strong unsettling sensation, as if the talisman is turning my head inside out, or a dream is replacing my waking life. It takes all my will power just to let it fall from my fingers and onto the off-white cloth. This object is so cold.

"You feel its power?"

"Yes," I answer, "oh yes. How did you acquire this... this... demonic object?"

"It came at the price of the life of one of my crew."

"What?"

"Let me explain. I had no choice. This was an expedition of exploration, my friend. Language was a barrier, we were not equipped for war, and we were outnumbered by tribesmen armed with harpoons. They led away one of my crew while their shaman gave me the talisman. By the time I realized what had happened, it was too late. Later, the shaman and a group of warriors led me away. I feared for my life, but it turns out they only wanted me to witness their barbaric ritual." He looks down at the blue tiled floor and takes a deep breath. "They sacrificed him."

"You saw it?"

"Yes. The Skraelings, clad in white furs, gathered in a circle. In the circle's middle there was a hole in the ice, a pit, with a big pile of excavated ice next to it. Around the circle's circumference were several ice sculptures. Eventually I discovered their true nature."

I already suspect how this will end but encourage Al-Balkhi to go on with his story.

"They pounded seal skin drums and played mad, whistling music on flutes made from human thigh bones. They danced and spun in frenzied circles- men, women, children- everyone hopping and jumping and shouting- and then two tribesmen led my crewman to the center of the circle. My crewman's eyes were glassy, and he moved slowly, as if in a dream. He must have been drugged. They lowered him into the pit and then covered him. They buried him alive."

"They froze him," I say.

He nods. "The same two tribesmen approached me, and I nearly panicked, but they took me by the arms and led me past the ice sculptures and back to *The Reunion of Broken Parts*. When I passed the sculptures, I realized..."

"Go on."

"The sculptures were frozen bodies from previous sacrifices. They posed the victims on pedestals, blocks of ice, and they intended to add my crew member to their statuary. I returned to *The Reunion of Broken Parts* and informed my crew. The Skraelings gathered on the shore in front of their ice huts and waved to us as we departed. I took my revenge and punished them with Greek Fire. God is great."

"You burned them?"

Al-Balkhi does not answer. Of course, he burned them. Greek Fire is an alchemist's dream. It combines naphtha and quicklime in a volatile mixture which ignites when combined with water. Fire and water. And now the talisman rests before me. "What is this thing called?"

"The tribesmen called it an Old One. They feared it and dreaded it. Do you want me to destroy it?"

"No... no. It is disagreeable, yet compelling. May I keep it?"

The explorer nods. "If anyone can learn from it, it is you. Return it to the Caliph when you are finished with your research."

After Al-Balkhi departs I re-light the candle, close the shutters, and return to my desk. The nightmarish object rests before me, a heavy malignant presence. Should I keep it? To do so feels wrong. It feels like a transgression, an act of heresy. Some of the more pious students in the House of Wisdom might see it as a graven image, although it resembles no known creature or pagan god. Those pious students might demand I destroy it. Perhaps the ivory carving is an image of a demon, or some sort of elemental deity from India or China. Pali texts translated into Arabic over a century ago describe strange beings, deities personifying earth, air, fire, water, and the quintessence, and yet, this particular ivory figurine comes from the far

north, not the lands of Persia or China, and I can discern no relationship between it and the five elements, other than the five starfish-shaped arms and the five sided symmetry of the body. Perhaps the figure really is an Old One, or its ghost.
I should destroy it right now, or at least wrap it in cloth.

And then, to my surprise, I find myself clutching the ivory carving in one hand. I tell myself it will inspire me, but how did it end up in my hand in the first place? With my free hand I pick up the quill, dip it into the lampblack, and poise it over the blank page, and then, in an act not of my own volition, I put the quill down. The cold wastes of the far north feel like they are right here in my study, emanating from the talisman to surround and envelop me. On impulse- or rather, compulsion- I pour bluish-black lampblack over the figurine and touch it to my bared right bicep. The contact freezes my skin and I scream, yet I do not stop pressing the talisman into my flesh. Cold white vapor rises and curls around my fingers.
At that moment a tremor shakes the Palace of Wisdom. The earthquake's rippling wave races through the blue tiled floor, as if the

real world is being distorted by an invisible power. The last thing I hear before I pass out is a cry from the street: "Look! The Tigris is flowing backwards!"

When I awake I am alone. Upon my bicep is the tattoo of the talisman. The unholy object is once again wrapped in its soft white cloth, although I do not remember putting it there. Dust motes swirl in the yellow candlelight. In one hand I still hold the quill.

At the edges of perception, a strange shrill noise like the buzzing of some nocturnal insect fills my ears. It grows louder until it degenerates into a mad, whistling, piping music, and out of the corner of my eye eerie contorted shadows wave and dance *in-between* the dust motes.

I know what to write. The Book, *Al Azif*, practically composes itself with words from beyond sanity's borders:

> Ghosts walk unseen in cold and lonely places. We heard their chill voices, although we could not see their shapes. They shrieked and gibbered in howling winds; they danced between tendrils of falling snow. When seasons changed the ghosts followed the cold. They followed it deep underground, beneath the icy depths of Kadath. Now the earth cracks and moans with the burden of their being. The cold wastes know them, but what do we know of the cold wastes? Of this we are sure: the ghosts have broken through before, and they

will break through again. Cold follows warmth just as winter follows summer, but when *their* winter comes again, warmth will not return. They shall break through and envelop our warmth in their madness, and then the cold ghosts shall hold dominion over all.

From the notes of Professor George Angle

The Arab Text

According to records, an Arabic copy of *Al Azif*- better known as the *Necronomicon*- was created in Baghdad shortly after the Abbasid Caliph, al-Mutadid Billah, died from dissolution in 902. A.D.

The copy was carried to Córdoba and the Library of al-Hakam II by the great Persian explorer and scientist, Abu Zayd al-Balkhi. That copy burned in 975 A.D. during one of the periodic outbreaks of religious fervor and opposition to 'rational science.'

The original Arab text burned when the Mongols sacked Baghdad in 1285.

From the notes of Professor George Angle

Commonalities appear throughout the history of the talisman and *Al Azif*, better known as the *Necronomicon*. In general, their appearance coincides with outbreaks of extreme violence; for example, the burning of the Jewish translation of the *Necronomicon* occurs at the same time as the crucifixion of the Jewish Vizier in Granada in 1066, followed by the expulsion of Jews from the Caliphate; and the burning of the Madrassa Library in Granada in 1499 by the Spanish Inquisition's Grand Inquisitor, Cisneros, is followed by the expulsion of the Muslims. Repeatedly, the appearance of the talisman and The Book coincide with rising dreams of national and religious supremacy. Again and again, the exceptionally violent acts surrounding the talisman and The Book are justified in the belief they will usher in yet another Golden Age for whatever nation or religion is in ascendance at that time.

Dr. Henry Armitage, author of the classic 1927 treatise *Notes toward a Bibliography of World Occultism, Mysticism, and Magic*, and I have identified other commonalities:

Fire

Earthquake

Explosives

Crevasses

Tidal Waves

Whirlpools

Horses

Deer

Insectile buzzing

Greek mythology, including the legend of Atlantis

Distortion of time and physics

Similar male and female personalities echoing through different times and settings

And most of all, the sensation of being cold

The commonalities resemble an allegory full of symbols and metaphors.

In addition to his academic expertise, Dr. Armitage also happens to be an avid philatelist- a stamp collector- and he has pointed out examples of similar allegories in the postage stamps of the British Empire as it became more and more violent; for example, the 1913 issue of the olive brown 2sh6, carmine rose 5sh, and blue 10sh stamp depicts "Britannia Rule the Waves," with the allegorical figure of Britannia as a charioteer, much like Poseidon. She carries a trident and a shield with a Union Jack coat of arms on it. A brace of hippocampi- mythological creatures that are half horse, half fish- pulls the chariot. The Barbados Colonial Seal issue of 1916 provides another good example. It shows the hippocampi pulling the chariot again, with Britannia as the charioteer, but this time a Latin motto has been added: "Et penitus toto regnantes orbe Britannos," which means "And the British rule throughout the world." The allegory and its symbols disappear from British and colonial postage shortly after the catastrophic violence of the Great War.

Last observation: Dr. Armitage says my name influences my writing. According to him, I make everything related to the talisman and The Book a mere *angle*, as if it were nothing more than a personal perspective on events.

From the notes of Professor George Angle

The Hebraic Text

Another Arab copy appeared in Granada in the early 11th century. At that time, Granada was a center for Jewish scholarship, and it is likely a Hebraic translation was created. However, the Muslims of Granada massacred the Jews and crucified the last Jewish Vizier, Joseph ibn Naghrela, in 1066. The Hebraic copy was burned at the time of his crucifixion on December 30th, 1066.

As of 1285 only two texts are known to exist: the Latin and the Arabic copies of *Al Azif*, in the great Madrassa Library in Granada.

⍰

The Madrassa Library

Granada, Spain 1499

The Madrassa Library fire rages. A crowd mills about in the market square, shouting and pointing and jeering at two desperate Saracen students fleeing the labyrinthine building. A toothless old man trips one of them. Some women grab and yank at another scholar's robes. The crowd slows the unarmed men enough for the guards to surround them, and without ceremony, the guards execute the Saracens on the spot.

Another scholar stands on the ledge of an upper story window. Black smoke billows past him as the crowd roars for him to jump. Tongues of orange flame finally touch his clothes and light his hair, and he has no choice; he plunges to the flagstones as the crowd cheers. The fall does not kill him, but he is badly injured and unable to rise. The guards execute him, too.

It is an immense conflagration. Now, let me say, I regret any loss of knowledge, for knowledge reflects God's glory. It is in that spirit that I have ordered all medical texts be spared. The rest must burn, along with the defenders of the Madrassa. And yet, these defenders arouse my curiosity. Most Saracens have already submitted to forced conversion or fled Spain, but these scholars do not act like typical Moors or Jews. There are not many of them and they know nothing about fighting, or tactics, but still they resist with violent rage. I believe they belong to a sect. A unique tattoo identifies its adherents. I *will* protect my flock from them.

I am Fray Francisco Jiménez de Cisneros, Archbishop of Toledo, confessor to Queen Isabella, and humble servant of King Ferdinand II. Next to the King and Queen, I am the best hope for salvation of my fellow Catholics in this world and in the next, may it please God. Today I am dressed for this formal occasion, the destruction of the last great repository of Arabic knowledge in Spain and perhaps the world. My rich red robe, soft white shoes, and white miter with gold trim announces my high position and social superiority, while the hooked crosier carried in my left hand lets Christians know I am a shepherd for their flock; in the eyes of our Savior, I am one of the flock, too. My stern features- my long nose, my narrow face- make many uncomfortable, but in truth, they are more intimidated by my reputation for rectitude and austerity than my title; at least, I would like to think so.

My lofty title never fails to astound me. How on earth have I become an Archbishop? After all, I was raised in poverty. I attended university and joined the priesthood. At one point, I even switched monastic orders, a very impolitic thing to do. But I am not ambitious. Thanks to my spiritual strength, granted by God, I have always been able to resist the lure of power and wealth and its attendant creature comforts. Neither greed nor the pleasures of the flesh tempt me, and this aura of incorruptibility has served me well. To this day, I sleep on the ground to remind myself of my humble beginnings, even though I am 63 years old. Like most monks- or, should I say, some monks- I am honest. I do not seek power for myself nor engage in petty court intrigues. So how did I advance to become confessor to the Queen? The answer is simple: selfless devotion. I serve Catholicism, King and Queen. What makes me different is my devotion to knowledge. I am a patron of Spanish humanists and promoter of mystical devotion, including the mystery of the Father, Son, and Holy Ghost, as well as the mystery of angels, for every angel is terrible.

The crowd has turned into a mob. Our savior says, 'the meek shall inherit the earth,' but there is nothing meek about them right now. They are poor, it is true, circling the square's periphery as if circling the edge of a whirlpool like so much flotsam and jetsam; yet I still stand at the spiritual and physical center of Granada, so there is hope. They should be thinking of their souls, but the fire has stoked their bloodlust, and they want more, especially the women and children. Ashes from burning books float down upon their heads like gray snowfall. The ashes fall upon my red robe and white leather shoes, too. The Madrassa burns. A puff of wind blows a small drift of ashes against my feet. *Ashes to ashes, dust to dust.*

The guards drag the last defender across the flagstones and bring him to me, followed by the crowd. Although most of the fight has been beaten out of him, the sole survivor of the Madrassa still has a wild look in his eyes. It takes four guards just to restrain him. His robe, once white, is now stained with sweat and blackened with soot. He looks like a Moor, with dark skin, black hair, and the voluptuous face of a decadent, but he does not behave like any Moor I have ever seen. Perhaps he is a lunatic. Two other guards stand nearby, each holding a thick, heavy book bound in black leather, with metal hasps. Nearby, a toothless old woman bites into a red pomegranate and the juice runs down her chin. I always thought it was curious that 'Granada' is the word for 'pomegranate.' The old woman spits the black seeds at the prisoner and says something, but her speech is so garbled I cannot make it out.

I gesture towards the prisoner with the crook of my crozier. "What is your name?" I ask.

"Arturo Tintorera," he responds.

"Tintorera? You are a dyer?"

"My name means 'dyer' but that is not what I do. I am Chief Librarian for the Madrassa Library."

"Your father was a dyer?"

"Yes."

"We have something in common. We both come from humble origins."

The head guard, a short crass man named D'Adelante, steps forward. "Your Excellency? We found this in his robe." He holds up an object wrapped in an off-white cloth. The cloth is wet. Apparently, the prisoner thought soaking it would protect it from fire.

"What is this?" I ask.

Tintorera gives a harsh laugh. "Unroll it and find out."

I nod to the head guard and from the unrolled cloth he produces a small ivory talisman. I have seen these before. Barbarians in the far north carve figures like these from bones and the teeth of whales, but not like this one. D'Adelante spits on the flagstone and hands the disconcerting object to me. It is incredibly cold to the touch. Not even exposure to the wet cloth could make it this cold. As for the talisman's shape, it looks like no creature I have ever seen, an impossible combination of a sea star, cactus, and beetle. It is bizarre and yet somehow incredibly compelling. This sudden, inexplicable compulsion helps me understand its nature: this talisman is magical, and therefore dangerous. I turn my head away and close my eyes while enclosing it in one fist. I take a deep breath to compose myself.

"Tintorera! I have seen this figure before." Using my staff, I address another guard named Grasso who is helping restrain the prisoner.

"Roll up his sleeve," I demand.

On the prisoner's right bicep is an ink tattoo shaped like the talisman.

Tintorera favors me with a ghastly smile.

"You are a member of a sect," I say.

He shrugs.

"You identify your fellow adherents with this tattoo."

"There are no more adherents, just me."

"Your false god failed you," I note with some satisfaction. Even as I speak the talisman seems to grow even colder. It pulses with barely contained magic.

Tintorera looks surprised, and then chuckles to himself. "You have no idea what you are talking about." The surrounding crowd mocks him with laughter and cruel jokes. Fights and arguments break out. He ignores them and focuses on me. "You feel it in your fist, don't you? I know you do. Drop that crosier. Press the talisman into your right bicep," he challenges.

It is tempting.

Some criticize me for my self-confidence, inflexibility, and even fanaticism. They consider these traits to be drawbacks. I know they do. And yet, my so-called flaws come to my rescue, and enable me to resist temptation.

I know what to do. In a moment of divine inspiration, I purposefully uncurl one finger at a time, and finally drop the ivory talisman to the flagstones. I grind it under my heel, to no effect. My shoes are too soft. Using the butt of my crozier, I pound the talisman into the stone, and with the first blow an unholy buzzing fills the broad square, a rising demonic hum as if from some angry nocturnal insect. I strike the talisman with my staff again and again, and with each blow, the buzzing grows louder and higher in pitch. The crowd falls silent in superstitious dread. Some freeze, while others fall to their knees and make the sign of the cross. My breath comes in gasps and the roar of my own heartbeat fills my ears. The demonic howling crescendos as I pulverize the talisman into powder.

The prisoner appraises me with a frank gaze. "I doubt you know what you just did. Few men have that kind of strength, especially in the presence of that book- two of them!"

I am still breathing too hard to answer. With one hand I smooth the front of my red robe.

He gives a nasty laugh. “You will see the talisman again in your dreams.”

The disrespectful tone pushes one of the guards on edge. He raises a truncheon to strike the prisoner. I quickly intervene before the guard can swing and I wave him off, and turn my attention to Tintorera.

“You are in no position to mock me, Chief Librarian.” I gesture for another guard to bring me one of the heavy books. Tintorera struggles feebly, but the guards restrain him. “Was it all for this?” I ask.

He gives up the struggle. “Yes. That is the last existing Arabic copy of *Al Azif*. I am its custodian.”

“I see. There are no other copies?” I question him.

“Not anymore. Not in Arabic.”

“What happened to the others?”

He scoffs. “You burn books, and then want to know more about them?”

The mere sight of this book leaves me shaking, and the effect is even worse with the talisman nearby. The mob growls with anger and anticipation. They want violence, but I must know more. "Indulge me, Tintorera. After all, you are the sole survivor of your cult."

"Very well." He lowers his chin and shifts his weight from one foot to another. "At the beginning of Islam's Golden Age a scholar wrote *Al Azif*. A copy was destroyed in 1285 when the Mongols of Hulagu Khan sacked Baghdad." He lets his attention wander towards the burning library, hoping I will follow his gaze and take the inferno here as a personal rebuke for what happened back then, as if I have anything to do with the depredations of Chinese barbarians! "The Mongols razed the House of Wisdom," he continues. "As for the books, they threw them in the Tigris. It is said the river ran black with ink, and red with the blood of scientists."

"There was another book?"

"Of course. An Arabic copy was brought to the Library of al-Hakam II in Córdoba by a great explorer, Al-Balkhi. That copy burned in the sack of Córdoba in 975. The other Arabic copy came here, to Granada."

"When?"

"About 500 years ago."

"The Jews ran the city back then. Did they make a Hebraic translation?"

"Maybe. If they did, none survived. The Muslims massacred the Jews in 1066. Every trace of Jewish scholarship was wiped out."

"Good."

He tosses his head in the direction of the book held by the other guard. "That is the only other one- a Latin translation."

"And what manner of book is it?" I ask him.

"A medical text."

He lies. I know it. Sometimes these Saracens evade. Other times, they plead. There is no truth in them. In the past, Muslims and Jews lied about their conversions to the faith, even after being imprisoned. It took extreme methods of interrogation to arrive at the truth. Today I know how to deal with it. I address the guard holding the Arabic copy. "Start a bonfire in the middle of the square. Burn it."

The guards comply, and the crowd joins in. The pile of wood quickly grows, and soon burning boards from the Madrassa are added to it.

Tintorera grows more and more agitated. He begs the guard and the manic crowd not to do this. No one pays attention. Old men make wild gestures and shout instructions which the younger men ignore. Mothers clap as children dance around their skirts. The public bonfire is blazing now. One of the guards, Grasso, raises the heavy black Arabic text over his head and looks to me for a signal. I hold my right hand high, make a fist, and extend my index finger. The crowd sees my dramatic gesture and goes silent in anticipation of what will follow.

Tintorera breaks. "Please. You must not do this. The Book describes the Old Ones."

"Never heard of them." I continue holding my hand high.

"*Al Azif* contains all knowledge from the far north and the far south. It is the most valuable book in existence."

I nod to one of the guards restraining him. "Blasphemer," the guard sneers, and cuffs him on the back of the head.

Another guard punches him in the gut. "Watch your mouth, infidel."

The violence drives the crowd to a frenzy, but before the guards can beat him senseless or the mob tear him apart, I intervene in a loud voice. "The Bible needs no defense from men such as this." I stare at my raised index finger and hold the pose until everyone is watching, and then I dramatically drop my right hand. Tintorera stifles a sob. Grasso throws the Arabic text on the fire where it burns.

As it ignites a small earthquake strikes. Its wave ripples across the square, and a concussive boom reverberates like thunder even though there are no clouds in the sky. The bells in the cathedral toll with the motion, and then go silent.

It is time to appeal to the pride Tintorera takes in his role as Chief Librarian. My question is cruel, but I put it as kindly as possible, since I still need more information. "Tell me, Arturo, what of this other copy, this Latin copy; should I burn it too?"

"You must not. That is the last copy of *Al Azif*."

"*Al Azif*? That is Arabic. What does it mean?"

"It is the sound made by a buzzing insect at night."

"What is it in Latin?"

"The *Necronomicon*."

"What? You say the Arabic title refers to the sound made by an insect. That is *not* what *Necronomicon* means. It sounds Greek."

Appealing to his scholarly background helps Tintorera regain his composure. "You are correct, your Excellency. There is no Latin equivalent for the Arabic title."

"Is there a Greek text?"

"Not as far as I know."

"*Necronomicon*," I say to myself. "The Book of the Names of the Dead." I re-engage the prisoner. "Tell me, are the 'Named Dead' the same as the Old Ones?"

"They are the same and they are different."

The surrounding crowd grows restless. I know my flock. They are in no mood for riddles. They want to burn him at the stake. I will seek information one more time. "Very well, Librarian. Tell me about the Old Ones."

"Your Excellency, I mean no disrespect, but it is impossible for you to understand the Old Ones without the tattoo of the talisman."

"Is that some sort of initiation rite? Do you worship the Old Ones?"

He shakes his head in frustration. "You do not understand."

"'Thou shalt have no other gods before me.' Do you know that commandment?" Tintorera defiantly stares at me. He knows the punishment for idolatry in both Islam and Christianity is harsh. He must also suspect he is not long for this world. "What do the Old Ones look like?" I ask.

"Their appearance varies. There is more than one kind. There are many and they are one."

"Describe one."

"You saw the talisman. It represents one form at one stage."

"I have seen and heard enough. Arturo Tintorera, out of respect for your love of knowledge, I would like to offer you one last chance for salvation. Will you renounce Islam and accept the Lord into your life?"

"If I do, will you spare my life?" he asks.

I shake my head sadly. The crowd roars its approval. Some are already building up the bonfire for a finale.

For the briefest moment, Tintorera screws up his face in hatred, but the expression quickly passes. Tintorera stands straight. "You know nothing. But I can change that. Take my life, if you must, but The Book is more important. The Old Ones and their ghosts do not care whether the text is in Arabic or Latin, or whether custodianship falls to the Christians or Saracens or Jews. That does not matter. Take The Book to your King. Its knowledge will save your country and even help you find Atlantis. It will make Spain the richest, greatest nation in the world. Take it to your King. Do this, and the end of the Golden Age of Islam will signal the beginning of the Golden Age of Spain.

No doubt he is lying, but his cult no longer poses a threat. It is gone. We have exterminated the brutes, save this one Librarian, and I have personally crushed the talisman. Only this one thick black tome remains, and its knowledge is now in Latin, not Arabic. Keeping it will add to the glory of crown and country, and soon the flag of Granada, the flag showing two green branches and a red pomegranate upon a white field, will proudly fly over a new empire. I take this book now to King Ferdinand.

From the notes of Professor George Angle

The Danish Text

Dr. Henry Armitage brought the following passage to my attention. He suggests the *Necronomicon* might have appeared in Copenhagen in the late 12th century. Some phrases from The Book resemble *The Danish History of Saxo Grammaticus*, such as the references to "monsters on horseback" and a "scowling horde of ghosts."

> Monsters on horseback gallop through the void. They careen through the abyss, and then leap from their nightmare and into our dreams to warn us; with aspects too grim to behold, the demons forbid us to cross the accursed river into their undiscovered country, even as they ride into our own. The monsters gather the reins of their mounts and call forth cold gales and blowing snow, while a scowling horde of ghosts draws near, and scurries furiously through the wind, bellowing drearily to the stars.

Mortlake Library by the River Thames

London

December 1589

The day is cold and gray and damp, and the River Thames flows backwards with the incoming tide. It flows from the ocean past Southend and London, past Mortlake and this ruined library, and upstream towards Reading and Oxford.

Most of you do not know me. My name is Edward Dyer and I am 46 years old. Some call me an ornament of the court. That is not true. I am a poet. Others whisper that I am the Queen's secret lover. That bit of slander is not true either. It is rumor spread by courtiers jealous of my appearance, for I am a handsome man, with light brown hair, gray eyes, and sharp yet regular features. More importantly, I am a bibliophile, which makes this damage to the rare and valuable books of Mortlake Library all the more distressing. The window has been shattered, allowing the misty rain to dampen some of the books and papers strewn across the floor; between the vandals and the water damage this represents an inestimable loss of knowledge. Ah, the cost! This was the largest private collection of books in England; not only that, someone dug a hole in the floor. Obviously, they were looking for something. Whatever it was, it is gone now, if it was ever there in the first place. The nearby fireplace is filled with gray ash and partially burned pages. Alas!

A ferryman rows his empty, rust-colored skiff past Mortlake and up the Thames. Did the vandals use his boat to reach the library? It seems unlikely. A miniature Union Jack flies from the bow, and most likely the vandals were not English. The ferryman is alone and rows with his back to the bow, so that he faces aft. Through the cold mist I can discern his unkempt beard, dirty greasy clothes, and blue-gray eyes. He looks like the mythical ferryman from Greek mythology, Charon, who takes the dead across the river Acheron and into Hades. That makes me even more nervous, so I jingle the silver coins in my pocket. In mythology, the Greeks placed a coin in the mouth of the deceased to pay for passage. Ah, the cost. It does not seem possible the ferryman could hear the jingling coins from that far away, but he flashes a hostile glance my way before redoubling his efforts on the oars. Soon he disappears into the mists, and I am left standing alone in the middle of this ruined library.

Before relating how that came to be, I should introduce the owner of Mortlake Library and my good friend, Doctor John Dee. While you may not know me, you probably know him; however, you need to be aware of some of his secrets.

How should I describe him? One would naturally imagine a man known as the Queen's Conjuror would be a fearsome fellow, dark and dour, but nothing could be further from the truth. Dee is happy and optimistic. How anyone can translate Euclidian mathematics in his spare time and still be happy and optimistic is a mystery to me.

As for his appearance, he is tall and slender, with rosy cheeks and hazel eyes. His most remarkable feature is his long, immaculately manicured white beard. I suppose it goes with the occupation. He shows it off by wearing a black robe with draping sleeves, which make even everyday gestures seem dramatic. Of course, these are appearances. Officially Dee is Her Majesty's scientific advisor, but in truth, he is the most powerful magician in Europe.

The court of Elizabeth I dotes on Doctor John Dee for good reason. Last year, the realm faced a terrible threat, an invasion from the Spanish Armada. That Catholic Armada would have crushed us. It would have put a Papist on the throne, ended the happy connection of Her Majesty's head to her body along with the rest of us, and terminated dreams of a Golden Age for the British Empire. Sir Francis Drake delayed the Armada with a series of victories, which was a notable achievement, but all he did was buy time. The Spanish Armada never reached English shores because of Dee.

Here is a secret: Dee single-handedly defeated the Armada. He cast a spell. He cursed them. He called up a monstrous storm and wiped those warships from the face of the earth.

Do not doubt this. I know. I was there. I watched him do it. Others saw it, too. It was simply incredible. Dee conducted a ritual in May 1588 in Winchester Cathedral. Many courtiers and the Queen's inner circle attended the rite, including Sir Francis Bacon; the Second Earl of Essex, Robert Devereux; his confidant, the young MP Francis Bacon; the first Earl of Leicester and my patron at the time, Robert Dudley; and my young friend, Kit Marlowe. The Queen presided over the ritual from her Coronation Chair, a warn, ornate, high-backed affair with its seat resting atop the Stone of Scone, better known as the Stone of Destiny, which once served as a portable altar for the Scots. (I often wonder how the Scots feel about English monarchs celebrating their crowning moment by parking their royal arses on Scotland's national symbol).

Now, where was I? Ah yes. The rite in Winchester Cathedral. What a scandal! No one wanted to talk about it afterwards, but we all know what happened. We all stared like a pack of slack jawed yokels when Dee cast his spell. He stood in the middle of a circle of a dozen off-white skulls and candles, chanting in an unknown language while the white-hot candles sparked and flared, erupting like so many volcanoes. Strangest of all, the skulls chanted along with him. The Queen and others believed Dee and the skulls spoke in tongues. A skeptic would observe skulls do not have tongues in the first place, but Dee claims both he and those skulls spoke in the universal language of angels. To this day the ghostly sound of those skulls haunts me.

Dee called up a towering wave in the North Irish Sea. From the perspective of those Spanish ships of war, it must have looked like the White Cliffs of Dover coming right at them.

The bloated bodies of Spanish seamen washed up on British shores for months afterwards.

Ah, Drake and Dee... They always worked well together. Both were navigators and cartographers at heart. Drake favored the physical realm of maps and routes, while Dee the metaphysical realm, but really, are they so far apart? Who can say where one stops, and the other starts? Dee- or should I say 007- was great with riddles.

Perhaps I should explain that reference. Dee was a remarkable cryptographer, and in his coded messages, Dee identified himself as 007. His penchant for secrecy and spy craft led him to establish a military intelligence network for the Queen. He was always pushing for ways to decode this world and the next, and so he was always pushing for voyages of discovery. Drake was more than willing to participate in secret missions.

Unknown to everyone other than the Queen and the Earl of Leicester, Dee gave Drake a secret assignment: voyage to the South Pacific and find Atlantis.

Plato described the fabulous city in a dialogue. It was beloved by Poseidon, a god of the ocean, earthquakes, horses, and more. According to Plato, Poseidon's city developed unrighteous power. Zeus, a god with a strong sense of irony, sent an earthquake to sink the city into the sea.

Dee believed there was more to the story, based on his strange communications with the angels in their universal language; at least, that is what he once said to me: 'every angel is terrible.' I believe he meant angels are terrifying. According to Dee, the angels told him how to find the sunken city by scrying with a hand mirror. Dee's alchemical skills came into play. Using quicksilver, orichalcum, and obsidian, Dee created the mirror and divined the location of Atlantis.

What is orichalcum? What is scrying?

Orichalcum is a yellowish-orange metal which flashes and glows red from within. According to Plato, it formed the inner ring walls surrounding Atlantis. The metal has not been seen since ancient times, and only an alchemist can produce it now.

As for scrying, that is a magical process. A person stares into a reflective medium- say, a mirror- and sees visions. The Spanish Catholics condemn this kind of thing as witchcraft, by the way. Like alchemy and fortune telling, it is easy to fake, and attracts all kinds of frauds and charlatans.

Dee, however, is no fraud. He is no charlatan. He is the Queen's Conjuror and scientific advisor for good reason.

While scrying with his mirror, Dee identified the geographical coordinates of Atlantis with great precision: 48°52.6′S 123°23.6′W. He placed it at a point called the Pole of Inaccessibility, also referred to as the Point of No One. He gave the position to Drake, and Drake sailed to the Southern Pacific.

A flash of light comes from the direction of the Thames. From outside the broken window, down by the riverbank, a small ghostly globe of light follows the current upstream towards Reading. The globe is an ignis fatuus, a will-o-the-wisp. Travelers follow them into marshes, become lost, and disappear in the trackless wastes. The pull of this one tempts me, but I resist, and remember I am working with Doctor John Dee. When weird events happen, Dee is probably close by. Speaking of Dee, where is he? He should have been here by now. It will not go well for me if the Spaniards return here before him. Of course, it will not go well for him either. The Spanish know Dee. They know what he did to their Armada. Well, with any luck, the eerie will-o-the-wisp will attract the Spaniards who ransacked Mortlake and draw them into cold water so that they drown, too.

As for those coordinates...

Drake sailed as close to them as he dared, but what he found in the Southern Pacific differed a great deal from what was described by Plato. There was no city. There were no concentric walls of brass and tin around the city, no red flash of orichalcum from the inner rings; instead, the city was a negation, a hole in the ocean, an enormous whirlpool like the one caused by the monster Charybdis in the *Odyssey,* only this maelstrom was in the middle of the Southern Pacific. At the funnel's bottom it was a swirling non-Euclidean nightmare, a jumble of geometrically impossible blocks of rotten greenish basalt piled one upon another with no recognizable structure; it was a bad dream, the antithesis of a city. Its malignant aura made a closer approach and inspection of its structure impossible.

From the sullen Thames a cool breeze ripples the water and momentarily parts the mist covering the long muddy lawn. It comes through the broken window, stirring the folds of the red and green drapes. An absurd thought crosses my mind: *Those curtains look like the northern lights*. Oddities often occur in Dee's presence. Speaking of which, Dee and Kit were supposed to be here by now. Where are they? The dampness chills my bones, so I wrap my cloak tighter, shift my weight from one foot to another, and shiver. That obsidian mirror Dee uses for scrying rests face down on the heavy wooden desk. I know better than to flip it over and gaze into its silvery surface, or even touch it. Apparently, the vandals who ransacked this place knew not to touch it, too. They were looking for something, and clearly it was not the mirror.

The light puff of wind sends some papers tumbling across the stone floor, and a map comes to rest at my feet. What is this place? It resembles no land that I know of. At first, I think it must be an island, but it has geographical features too large for a mere island. No, this is a white, roughly circular continent with one long arm extending into a featureless expanse- presumably, an ocean. The coast is limned in black. A chain of volcanoes extends up the arm and into the interior, but otherwise, the land mass is blank. One word has been scrawled in red across the blank space: Kadath.

Ah, Dee. Always writing in code.

Private codes from 007 for privateers like Sir Martin Frobisher and Sir Francis Drake were common. Frobisher sailed on an expedition to the far north. He returned from his voyage with some rotten, greenish-black basalt from *Meta Incognita* and a handful of charred skulls. He claimed the basalt contained gold. This caused a sensation, but in fact, the sample contained no such thing. It was merely iron pyrite- truly, fool's gold. Any honest assayer would have known that, but then again, 'honest assayer' is an oxymoron. Iron pyrite is supposed to be good for striking a spark, but this sample was good for nothing whatsoever.

All the foolishness about gold overshadowed Frobisher's truly significant find: a magic talisman. When Frobisher brought it to court and presented it to the Queen, she refused to touch it. Who can blame her? The nightmarish idol pulsed with cold black magic. It looked like a nightmare, too, a demonic carving of a creature resembling a cross between a starfish, cactus, and beetle. Only one person in England could control such a dangerous artifact, and that was Doctor John Dee. Custody of the powerful figurine fell to him, and he concealed the fell object here, in Mortlake Library.

Footsteps approach down the long hallway leading to the library. Is it Dee, or the vandals?

"Who's there?" I query bravely.

A young man in a black cape rushes through the open door. He has wild, reddish-brown hair and sports a trim mustache and beard, like so many of today's rakes. Raindrops bead his hair and clothing, giving him a silvery sheen. "Good day, fellow Dyer. Only let's not die today, shall we? We need to go."

"Kit!" I exclaim. "What's going on? Where is Dee?"

"Right behind me," he says, glancing at the doorway. "Listen, we cannot stay here." He sways slightly and reaches for a bookshelf for balance. Kit is agitated and he is breathing hard, but I suspect he is swaying because he is drunk. It is not surprising. Christopher Marlowe has a reputation for immoral conduct and womanizing. Typical artist.

"Hello, Edward." Doctor John Dee greets me as he breezes into the library but stops in his tracks when the extent of the damage becomes apparent. Shocked by the mistreatment of this repository of knowledge, his lower lip trembles, and his normally cheerful features fall slack. He pulls himself together faster than I expected. "They are coming."

"The people who did this?" I ask.

"Yes," Dee and Marlowe answer simultaneously.

Dee mutters to himself as he picks up and discards books. "Where is it?" He crawls across the damp floor on his hands and knees, frantically going through the texts and manuscripts. *"Liber E, Liber Os... Liber Sipal."* He quickly examines them and randomly replaces them on the shelves. "Ah! *The Book of Soiga*." He hands the book to me and I carefully place it on a separate shelf.

"What is that?" Marlowe asks.

"A text of magic," I reply, "covering demonology, the genealogies of angels, astrology, labyrinths-"

"-Is that what we are looking for?" he interrupts.

"No," I answer curtly.

"We are looking for *Redeeming Time and Memory*," Dee clarifies.

I help Dee search while Marlowe stares into the distance. "Soiga," he observes, "is 'holy' spelled backwards in Greek- 'agios'." No doubt about it. Drunk or sober, Marlowe is sharp. Dee continues his frantic search. "Can't find it?" Marlowe asks. "I thought you were a magician."

"That's enough, Kit." I turn to Dee. "Ignore him, Doctor, he is in his cups."

If looks could kill, Dee would drop him like a stone. "Marlowe, I thought you were supposed to be a translator, or an artist, or *something*. Do you do anything other than drink ale? Be helpful, for once." He resumes sorting through the books on the floor, mumbling "drunk as a poet on payday."

Marlowe ignores him. "I *am* an artist, and an artist is a magician. I translate the world, just as an alchemist- like you, Dee- translates metals." Dee snorts, but Marlowe is just warming up. He throws his arms wide to encompass the entire room, including the books and papers on the floor, and speaks melodramatically like a professional actor, projecting his voice so that it fills every corner of the room.

> These metaphysics of magicians
> And necromantic books are heavenly:
> Lines, circles, letters, and characters-
> Ay, these are those that Faustus most desires

The man is a genius. I am a good enough poet to know it. "What is that from?" I ask.

"*The Tragical History of the Life and Death of Doctor Faustus*. A work in progress."

"*Doctor* Faustus?" I ask Marlowe, shooting a glance in the direction of Doctor John Dee, who is still crawling around the floor.

Marlowe smiles. "That's right. A doctor sells his soul for knowledge. He dabbles in black magic, believing books will save him from death and oblivion." Dee pauses long enough to give him another dirty look. If Marlowe and Dee keep going at each other this will end badly. To change the subject, I randomly pick up a book and open it to an illustration of constellations. It shows the strange stars of the southern sky. Another page shows faint stars, including the brightest southernmost star in the Southern Cross, Alpha Cruxis. It borders an area blacker than black. The caption reads 'The Coalsack Nebula.' The illustration is profoundly disturbing, an emptiness that fills me with dismay, but I never get the chance to bring up the subject. Marlowe has picked up the obsidian hand mirror from the desk and now gazes into its quicksilver depths. He tilts his head and looks astonished; without meaning to, he is scrying. His face goes slack, his eyes grow round, and his jaw drops.

"Kit!"

The mirror falls from his hand, but a diving Dee stretches to his full length and catches it before the mirror can hit the stone floor. Dee carefully places it on the desk, face down, and addresses Marlowe in a stern, clipped tone. "Do not touch that."

Marlowe snaps out of his nearly catatonic state and rapidly nods in agreement.

"What did you see?" I ask.

He draws a deep breath and shakes his head as if to clear it. "A vision."

"Go on."

"A world of ice. Falling snow. Shadows... dancing in-between swirling flakes. Unholy things, things that should never be seen. They're too cold. I saw a deep crevasse in the ice-"

"-Enough!" Dee loudly interrupts, and then lowers his voice. "You saw the angels. All that ale you imbibed protected you from the full impact of their terrible presence. Now, let's focus on the task at hand. Hand me that book."

"Angels?" Marlowe scoffs. "Those were no angels, Dee, not even fallen ones. They had nothing to do with heaven or earth. They were more like... ghosts."

"It is better not to talk about them," Dee declares.

Marlowe hands Dee a book and picks up another. He opens the text to an illustration of a plant. "What manner of book is this?"

Dee spares him a glance. "A pharmacopeia. It has the formulas for elixirs that let me handle The Book and the talisman without falling under their power. The potions also let me scry without going mad. Would you like one?"

"Thanks," Marlowe says, "but I'll stick with ale." He places the pharmacopeia on a shelf.

Dee picks up another book and shouts in triumph. "Ha! Here it is." He opens *Redeeming Time and Memory*, by Alihak. The inside of the book has been hollowed out to hide objects. Now it is empty.

"Gone!" Dee exclaims.

"What was in there?" Marlowe asks.

"The talisman," I answer. "Now it is in the hands of the mob."

"They ransacked the library," Dee adds. "They deserve the talisman."

"It was not a mob," Marlowe asserts. "The Spanish did this. The Inquisition."

"How do you know?" I ask.

"I followed them up the road towards Reading. They were gliding along, wrapt in brown mantles, hooded. They went into a pub."

"A pub? How *very* fortunate for you," Dee says sarcastically.

"Which pub?" I ask.

"The White Fire," Marlowe answers. "The monks sat at one long table. They spoke Spanish and caused a real ruckus. One of them was pressing an object into another's arm. It must have been painful. There was a lot of shouting."

"A pox on them." Dee shakes his head. "Well, now they are servants of the Old Ones and The Book. The important thing is to keep The Book away from the Spaniards."

"And any other bloody Papists," I added.

"True," Dee agreed. "The Spaniards will be back, you know. The talisman will draw them south, towards The Book."

Marlowe and I exchange looks. The hole in the middle of the stone floor is obviously a hiding place, and there are partially burned pages in the fireplace. "Where is it?" I ask Dee. "Where is The Book?"

He smiles, walks to the hearth, and removes two flat stones from the side of the chimney. Behind them is a compartment containing a thick text bound in black leather with metal hasps. “The *Necronomicon*,” he announces. “I keep it as close to a fire as I dare.” He runs his fingers through his long white beard, stares into the distance, and absent-mindedly mutters to himself. “The fire seems to dampen the call.”

“Dee,” I say, “if they realize they destroyed the wrong book-” I begin.

“-When,” he finishes.

“They will come back,” I continue. “They will be angry about falling for a ruse and they will want revenge. We are in great danger. The Spaniards may burn Mortlake to the ground.”

Dee shakes his head in sorrow. “When I was in Prague, I translated the *Necronomicon* into German for Emperor Rudolf. Once he understood its nature, he ordered it burned. I left before they could treat me to a good old-fashioned Bohemian defenestration.”

“A what?” I ask.

“Defenestration. They take you to a meeting hall high in Prague Castle, and throw you out the window. It is a long way down. In any case, they torched my German translation, but I brought the original back with me. Listen, we must save Mortlake. Her Majesty will surely provide guards for the Queen's Conjuror if I request them. And if they attempt to cross the ocean and return the talisman to Spain, I will curse them." Marlowe and I exchange glances. We both know what happened to the Spanish Armada. "But that won't be enough," Dee continues. "The Spanish monks are initiates of the talisman, and The Book will compel them with its call. We have to remove it from Mortlake and hide it somewhere safe."

"Where?" I ask.

Dee resumes grooming his beard. "A place that can suppress the call. We need a vortex of power."

"I know a place," I say, "but I will need help. Marlowe, you're young. Come with me. I'll need your assistance to move a heavy stone. Dee, see if you can flag the ferryman on his way downstream. And we'll need to pull some strings to get into this place without anyone knowing, other than the Queen."

Dee laughs. "I think I can guess. Winchester Cathedral."

"That's right. In the Coronation Chair, beneath the Stone of Destiny."

From the notes of Professor George Angle

In 1657, Oliver Cromwell and his New Model Army moved the Coronation Chair from Westminster Cathedral to Winchester Abbey for a ceremony. Obviously, The Book was not in the Chair at that time. If Cromwell's forces had found it the Puritans would have destroyed it on the spot, and the sensational discovery would have thrown the country into chaos. The most likely explanation is that descendants of Dee or Dyer removed it before the ceremony and tried to protect it by shipping the text to America, possibly by way of the island of Barbados.

According to unverified reports, the Spanish monks lost their talisman when a freak storm swamped their ship in the Bay of Biscay. All hands were lost. A new talisman from the north must have followed The Book to the New World at that time.

Two ships are likely candidates for transporting The Book to the New World:

The *Algebra*, a warship that doubled as a slaver, sailed from the Thames to Africa, to the Caribbean island of Barbados, and then on to the Port of Boston in 1656. The *Melissa*, a small freighter out of London, also sailed to the island of Barbados and then to Boston that same year. At the time, the island was notorious for the practice of voodoo. Later, a slave from Barbados, Tituba, was deeply involved in the Salem Witch Trials and accused of witchcraft.

A book burning took place in Boston's Market Square in 1656, shortly after the *Algebra* docked. A local colonial paper blamed a female passenger for "spreading sundry books, in which are contained corrupt, heretical, and blasphemous doctrines contrary to the truth of the gospel."

From the notes of Professor George Angle

In this recently discovered account, an adult woman from the 1700's, Sonny Green, wrote about her nightmarish experience as a teenager in South Reading, Massachusetts in 1693. This occurred shortly after the infamous Salem Witch Trials, but her account never made it into the public eye.

The language and spelling have been modernized for the convenience of the reader; however, the lack of religious references is not a result of editing. The account lacks the usual appeals to God, the Savior, and the Holy Ghost so typical of that time period. Unfortunately, there is no supporting evidence for her story, which is not surprising, considering records from the period are sparse. Her story was written decades after the fact; nevertheless, Sonny Green's account rings true. Why would she lie? And yet, questions abound. The story must be approached with caution, for clearly Sonny Green is an unreliable narrator. A person of the same name gave a testimonial in an advertisement which appeared in the *Arkham Gazette*. In it, she promoted the benefits of an elixir, laudanum, which was a tincture of opium and alcohol. The advertisement refers to a husband but does not name him. Sonny Green taught school in Peabody and died at an advanced age in the Arkham lunatic asylum. That does not necessarily mean she was mad or under the influence of opium when she wrote this.

South Reading, Massachusetts

May 1, 1693

My name is Sonny Green. This happened long ago, when I was young. Since then, I have heard about the Salem Witch Trials, but as far as I know, no account of the events at South Reading have ever been published. That is not surprising, since I am the only one likely to bring it up, and I have never spoken or written about it up until now. Up to that fateful day, my childhood was typical for a Puritan growing up on an inland plantation. Everyone was very religious. My family consisted of my Father, Mother, and three younger sisters. I did household chores and helped Mother with the girls. My main job was bringing water from the creek to our log cabin. My best friend, Antonia Wilcox, was like a sister to me, although we did not look much like each other. Antonia was beautiful and tall and willowy, with long brown hair and soft brown eyes, while I was short and not willowy at all, with curly brown hair and blue eyes. Antonia helped us with chores, too, and in turn, my mother taught her to read from the Bible. We all worked together and played together. My favorite memories are of playing with my sisters and best friend in that little creek.

Thanks to my Mother, my sisters and Antonia and I knew how to read. Antonia especially liked the Bible and writing poetry. She had an artistic temperament, despite living so far from civilized cities like Boston. She was sensitive and devout, even by Puritanical standards, and she often complained of bad dreams; in retrospect, I believe her faith made her brittle and more vulnerable, and that made her terrible experience with the sachem much worse. Since South Reading, I am no longer comforted by Christianity, but as I said, back then it played an important role in everything we did. Some, like Judge Bonnerville, probably took religion too seriously for their own good, to the point of fanaticism. He was a big, humorless man with pock-marked skin and a large gray drooping mustache who came from Arkham to give Sunday sermons. Most of us were too busy surviving on the edge of the civilized world to worry about fire and brimstone and angels. We were just a handful of families- the Dyers, the Widmarks, the Danforths, and the Kores- with a handful of cabins and a small church that doubled as a town hall. A few men, such as

Captain Marsh, and a dirty, foul-mouthed French trapper, LeGrasse, visited on occasion and brought news from other towns.

Captain Marsh was tall, with dark hair, dark eyes and heavy eyebrows, and he was as decent as a man could be. His wife and children lived in Arkham. Even though he was not an eligible bachelor, both Antonia and I had a crush on him. Was that so surprising, considering our age, and how few young men were available on the frontier?

LeGrasse, on the other hand, was middle-aged and portly and no taller than me, with flat blue eyes, short gray hair, and a ruddy complexion. The broken capillaries in his bulbous nose led me to suspect he imbibed- well, that, and the perpetual reek of hard liquor, not to mention the canteen on his belt that he refused to share with others. Life on an inland plantation was no place for anyone with delicate sensibilities, but LeGrasse was challenging even by our standards. He was incredibly profane. He wore dirty, greasy furs. He stank to high heaven. One would think a fur trapper would save the best furs for himself, but oh no, not LeGrasse. Despite his failings, he was valued for his superior hunting and tracking skills, and his decisive and even brutal manners gave others a sense of security.

He kept company with a pair of brothers, Wayne and Augustine Shipper. The Shippers were in their 30's. Like most people on the frontier, they could neither read nor write, but they possessed a kind of base cunning which served them well while hunting. Wayne was older and taller and had curly light brown hair, while Augustine had a darker complexion and bad teeth. Both were cynical and possessed lax moral characters. Augustine always asked inappropriate questions about "that young filly," my friend Antonia. They drank as much as LeGrasse but lacked his inner reserve of strength, which LeGrasse found in law and order. LeGrasse was curiously devoted to it yet stayed as far away as possible from the towns and cities where law and order were most necessary.

An inland plantation is an isolated place, so we depended on men like LeGrasse, Marsh, and Judge Bonnerville for trade and news of the outside world. They kept us in touch with villages like Salem, Andover, Lynn, Peabody, and Arkham. Those villages were to the east. To the west- nothing. A gloomy primeval forest stretched through ancient, eroded hills and eventually to the White Mountains. The forests used to be green and the fall colors were amazing, with lots of yellows and glowing reds, or so my parents told me, but the old growth trees had sickened and died from some sort of blight, to be replaced by stands of thin, starving aspens.

Following the creek downhill led to a marsh and the Great Pond. Today the Great Pond has a long Indian name- Lake Quannapowitt- but to us, it was always just the Great Pond. From time to time Antonia and I went there to fish. I remember the two of us hopping across the flat rocks in the creek, and laughing, and wondering about the boys in the villages to the east.

Following the creek uphill, from South Reading towards the mountains, was difficult. Tree trunks had fallen across it. Rounded stones and big mossy boulders forced crossings back and forth through the watercourse, so there was always a risk of turning an ankle, but despite those hazards, following the creek was still better than the alternative. Striking out across the trackless forests was dangerous for anyone, especially a young girl, partly because it was so easy to get lost, and of course, there were savages.

According to Judge Bonnerville, a local tribe used to live here, the Naumkeag. They were friendly and peaceful. Almost all of them died of a pox in the early 1600's, decades before we came to South Reading, but a few survived deep in the forest. According to LeGrasse, the survivors had a new sachem, a witch doctor, and they had started a new religion, some sort of ghost cult. Victims were supposedly taken by the sachem deep into the woods and never heard from again.

On the morning of April 29, 1693, Antonia and I went down to the creek to fetch water, and the savages were lying in wait. They chased us. I ran. One nearly caught me, but I threw a big rock and hit him in the face. I might have killed him. Perhaps I should thank the Lord for having enough strength to throw a rock that heavy, and for guiding it so that it felled the brute, but in truth, my strength came from fear, not faith. Although I escaped, the brutes captured Antonia and took her into the forest. I will never forget that filthy degenerate sachem grabbing Antonia by her long hair, or the way she screamed and flailed her arms as they dragged her away.

Captain Marsh, LeGrasse, the Shippers, and a few other trappers tracked them. They rescued Antonia, but the savages fled. Antonia was hysterical. Captain Marsh brought her back to South Reading by tying her onto a travois made of aspen trunks and dragging her. LeGrasse and the others pursued the sachem and his tribe. LeGrasse never talked about what happened, other than to mention a peculiar tattoo the savages wore on their right bicep. It seems they burned a bizarre image into their skin using a magical idol. In any case, I have no doubt LeGrasse and his men found the camp that same night and exterminated the brutes, because when they returned the next morning, several of the trappers carried bloody scalps on their belts. We never heard from that tribe again.

One of the trappers returned with a large book bound in black leather. I remember the man, a short fellow with a big nose and oily skin. His name was more distinctive than his appearance: Howard Philippe Amour-Artisanat. I also remember LeGrasse cursing the book, and saying "burn it," followed by a string of profanities, but Judge Bonnerville wanted to keep it.

The Judge called for a meeting the next day. I remember the exact date, May 1st, because I kept repeating '*Mayday, Mayday, Mayday*' to myself. I was feeling poorly that morning, so my mother gave me a tincture of laudanum before we left. My father took my mother's hand, and my sisters and I walked behind them to the small log cabin that served as a meeting place and church. Everyone attended, except Captain Marsh, who left for pressing business in Arkham.

We met a neighbor, Penny Kore, on the way. According to her, Antonia was suffering strange fits which Penny called "the disease of astonishment."

Judge Bonnerville had already raised a flag over the peak of the cabin, a red cross on a white field- Saint George's Cross. The sun was bright, but inside the windowless cabin it was dark, with only candles for illumination. Everyone crowded into the room. My mother and father and sisters stood in front, but I was feeling faint, so I stood in back by the open door for some fresh air. LeGrasse stood next to me, leaning against the door, probably because he was drunk. Judge Bonnerville faced the small gathering. On one side of him was a table with an unknown object resting upon it, covered by a white cloth. On the other side my friend Antonia was still tied to the upright wooden travois. She was bound and gagged. Manacles chained her skinny arms and legs to its rickety frame. She wore the same plain brown dress she had been wearing when she was kidnapped, but it had been ripped during her ordeal. Her hair was loose and disheveled, and she showed no awareness of us or her surroundings, or immodesty over her torn dress, only wild anger at being restrained. This anger went beyond hysteria. She seemed enraged, as if possessed by a malevolent spirit. Antonia thrashed against the hemp ropes. The wooden poles creaked, and the ropes strained as she struggled, but fortunately they held.

Judge Bonnerville addressed her. "Antonia Wilcox?"

She did not respond or even show any signs of recognition.

The judge fingered his lavaliere, a small silver cross that caught the soft yellow glow of the candlelight. "Antonia Wilcox, I am Judge Bonnerville. Can you hear me? What happened to you? Speak!"

Antonia twisted and threw herself from side to side.

"Are you possessed by a demon?" He eyed her speculatively and rubbed his chin. "Are you a witch? Blink once for yes, twice for no."

Her eyes darted about the room without focusing.

"Let her be!" her father cried. "My daughter is no witch!"

“Please,” her mother begged, her voice cracking with anguish. “She was taken by the sachem.”

Bonnerville glared at them. “Hold your tongues. There is more here than meets the eye.” He startled everyone by suddenly ripping away the cloth fabric from Antonia’s right arm, exposing her pale skin. Upon her bicep was a small, crude black tattoo. It looked like an impossible creature, a combination of cactus, black beetle, and five-armed starfish. “What is this?” Bonnerville roared. “Is this a demon?” Antonia wildly rolled her eyes but did not blink.

“The sachem did that to her,” I cried from the back of the room.

“Quiet, girl,” he said, and leaned over the table. “No doubt, someone else did this to her, but why did she try to hide it? We also found this.” With a dramatic flourish he pulled the white cloth away from the object on the table, revealing a thick black book with metal hasps, bound in weathered black leather. Up until now there had only been one book in the village, a Bible, but this was definitely not a Bible. Just looking at it made me feel uneasy, like my head was being turned inside out.

Antonia threw herself to one side so forcefully, she nearly knocked over the travois. The Shipper brothers stood on either side of her and held the wooden poles upright.

The judge leaned so close their noses nearly touched. "Where did this infernal text come from, Antonia Wilcox?"

Eyes wide with horror, she avoided his gaze and stared at the large book.

"Did the sachem show it to you?" he shouted. "Blink once for yes, twice for no."

She closed her eyes and gave a long, muffled moan.

"Should I remove her gag?" Wayne Shipper asked.

Bonnerville fingered his silver cross and appeared to consider the matter. "No. Not yet." He addressed Antonia again in a softer, more conciliatory tone. "This book came from Salem Village, did it not? An old woman brought it to the Naumkeag." He lowered his voice and spoke to the rest of us. "I spoke with the Chief Magistrate from Boston. He says the book came to Salem Village last year. One of the witches, Bridget Bishop, fled the Village and left it with the Naumkeag for safekeeping."

“Thou shalt not suffer a witch to live” one of my neighbors declared.

Bonnerville nodded his appreciation of the sentiment and favored us with a self-satisfied smile. “We are well on our way to a golden age for American theocracy. That witch has since been tried, convicted, and sentenced to hang. A job well done!”

He piously gazed towards the roof as if appealing to a higher authority. “Now, of course, we all know the Naumkeag are degenerate savages and cannot read.” He paused and abruptly pointed at Antonia. “But she can.” He picked up the book and waved it in front of her face. She tossed her head from side to side in a frantic effort to avoid looking at the black tome.

“Will you read to us from that book?”

She continued thrashing against her restraints.

“No?” Bonnerville continues. “Shall I?”

She blinked twice and violently shook her head from side to side.

He slowly opened the book. The gag stifled her scream.

At that same moment, a deep rolling boom came from the deep woods, a muffled noise like a distant thunderclap, or the rumble made by an earth tremor.

Inside the cabin, the temperature plunged. It felt as if my very soul had been surrounded by a shroud and froze. Others groaned, gasped, or covered their faces with their hands as the cold encompassed them. A few recited the Lord's Prayer. Mister Widmark yelled "They're too cold!" Out of the corner of my eye, I glimpsed... a force... something diabolical, dancing in the shadows cast by the flickering candlelight, something real, yet not of this world. I saw something that should *never* be seen.

Judge Bonnerville shook his head in confusion. "What manner of writing is this? Is it code? What language?"

"G** d*** it!" LeGrasse exclaimed and stormed the short distance to the front of the room. The rest of us were too shocked to move, but LeGrasse acted. He ripped the text away from the judge and slammed it closed on the table.

Bonnerville held his head in his hands as if awaking from a bad dream. "That book... Help me... it is demonic."

"Hand me that candle," LeGrasse demanded. The judge was too confused to respond, so the trapper shoved him aside. "Never mind." LeGrasse grabbed the candle and touched the small yellow flame to the corner of the book. At first, only a thin black wisp of smoke rose, but then the book burst into white-hot flame. LeGrasse recoiled from the fireball and staggered towards the open door and me. The brothers cackled and capered like madmen and set Antonia's dress on fire. Her father roared and charged, and they fell in a heap, punching and kicking while Antonia burned. My mother screamed 'stop it' over and over. Judge Bonnerville yelled "the valley of the shadow of death."

LeGrasse pushed me out of the cabin and followed behind me, and we ran. It was no longer sunny as a heavy bank of roiling gray clouds rolled over with frightening rapidity, followed by stronger and stronger wind gusts. An incongruous thought popped into my head: *"Looks like a Nor-easter.'* I quickly checked myself; this storm came from the south. Also, I had seen Nor-easters before, and this looked nothing them. Heavy clouds seemed to organize themselves, circulating about a central eye like a whirlpool, and drawing my gaze upwards towards the bottomless eye in the sky. I tripped over a boulder, scraped my knee, stood, stumbled, and ran some more. Thanks to the insulating properties of the laudanum I hardly noticed the injury. Buffeted by the furious wind, I fled that cabin, holding my arms in front of me to protect me from airborne branches. Where was LeGrasse? I spotted him holding onto a nearby tree trunk. And then the rain came down, and I lost track of the trapper. The rain pelted my skin so hard it hurt, and the temperature plummeted. It must have been well below freezing. A hurricane gust knocked me down again as a tremendous high-pitched whine came from the sky. It grew louder and louder, like an enormous bird or buzzing beetle diving towards me, and tinny, nonsensical words emanated from the manifestation: "pull up, pull up, pull up." I crawled through a downpour of hail; big trees cracked and fell like matchsticks. The high-pitched whine reached a deafening crescendo, and then, from behind me, a flash of light and an explosion came from the vicinity of the cabin… and that is my last recollection of the catastrophic event, for I passed out. As far as I know, my mother, father, sisters, Antonia, and the other residents of South Reading were still inside that cabin. When I came to my senses, I found myself staggering up the small creek towards the mountains, following a small ball of white light, a will-o'-the-wisp, that floated over the rocks and water. In my mind, I thought I was traveling downstream towards the Great Pond, but in fact I was traveling upstream. The crazy thing is that I could swear the water was flowing uphill. If I had continued following that will-o'-the-wisp I would have been utterly lost, but once I became conscious of it, the ball of light disappeared; now, the buzzing of insects filled my ears. I must have been mad. My only other clear memory was of a large stag that stood motionless by the watercourse and watched me scramble across the boulders.

LeGrasse rescued me. He tracked me and led me back towards the Great Pond. We passed the site where South Reading used to be. It was gone, gone, gone, wiped clear from the face of the earth. There was no sign of my mother and father, no sign of my sisters, or any of the other families. Not even fallen tree trunks littered the area surrounding where the cabin had once stood; the topsoil had been blown away, and it had been scoured clean down to the bedrock, with one exception: at the spot where the book and Antonia had been burned, there was a broad shallow crater filled with gray ashes and a single artifact, namely, the small silver cross that had belonged to Judge Bonnerville. LeGrasse wanted to destroy it. He claimed he found a magic idol at a Naumkeag camp site, and he believed the sachem used the idol for ghost cult initiations. He also claimed he stomped the object into a powder, and now he wanted to annihilate this cross, too, because he believed it held magical power. That seemed unlikely to me. It obviously did not help Judge Bonnerville. I refused to let him harm the cross, and after that LeGrasse refused to discuss it any further. After some hesitation, I pocketed it and brought it with me to Arkham.

At the time, the judge insisted Antonia was a witch working for demons. In retrospect, I realize what happened in South Reading had nothing to do with demons, or good and evil, or heaven and hell, or anything mentioned in the Good Book. What I witnessed convinced me this was the work of a malignant entity completely and utterly separate from such considerations, that a magical book of dark magic provoked it, and that a mysterious talisman initiated unfortunate victims like my friend, Antonia Wilcox, into its madness.

Recently I visited the site of South Reading, supposedly located near the towns of Salem, Andover, Lynn, and Reading. There is nothing there. The original village of Reading was located near the south shore of the Great Pond, Lake Quannapowitt, so South Reading should have been nearby.

A small creek empties into the lake, and using clues from Green's tale, the creek can be followed upstream through the marshes, and into the woods. I found a location that is almost certainly South Reading, but it is a bare field of gray boulders, and nothing grows.

Francis Thermonde

San Francisco, California
April 18, 1906

The nautilus shell and small brass horse vibrate and slide to one side of the coffee table ever so slightly, as if by magic.

My elderly host, the Southern Pacific Shipping magnate Jan Hippos, notices my alarm. He rolls back a sleeve of his silk purple bathrobe and holds up a frail hand, palm facing me. “Merely an earth tremor, Professor Angle. It is nothing- happens all the time. You get used to it.” He smiles reassuringly, but his long, equine face and large teeth make his expression disconcerting. The magnate leans forward from his plush coral chair and examines the thick tome before him. He lightly runs a palsied hand across his bald pate, and then touches the black leather cover, staring at the text in awe. He looks up at me. “Thank you. An English translation of the *Necronomicon*! What a wonderful addition to my collection.” He turns to my young companion, who holds a similar, much older text in his lap. “And thank you, Mr. Forth.”

Daniel dips his chin in acknowledgement. "You are welcome, sir." He places his text- the original Latin text- on the table next to the horse statue and shell. "Where would you like me to put your translation?"

The magnate indicates the tall, heavy bookshelf next to him. "Up there would be fine."

The shelves are stuffed with rare books about the occult. The available space is on the top shelf, and Daniel is short, so he stands on his tiptoes, and even jumps a little, in order to push the book into place. Unlike me, the young bachelor has removed his dark blue sack coat; still, he is reasonably well dressed in his slightly rumpled white shirt, navy vest and trousers, and black leather shoes, but jumping like that makes him look thoroughly undignified, and Jan finds it mildly amusing.

Daniel scans the titles before him. "You have a lot of Poe. I recognize this book. It's a first edition of a collection of his stories. I especially like *Descent into the Maelstrom*."

They share their enthusiasm for Poe's stories, but I am not a fan. The tall grandfather clock in the corner strikes 5:00 o'clock and gives me the opportunity to change the subject. "We appreciate your entertaining us at such an early hour."

Jan shrugs. "I have to admit, it is not every day I conduct business before sunrise, but in this case..." He produces a sheaf of paper currency from a pocket in his robe and hands it to Daniel. "I understand you have an early train to catch."

Ah, the cost. Daniel pockets our payment for translating such a dangerous text. Jan Hippos loaned us his Latin copy of the *Necronomicon*, the only one in existence. In exchange, we created one English translation for him and made a second one for ourselves, which we will take back to Miskatonic University. "Our horse and buggy is out front, but it can wait a few more minutes."

"Good weather for travel," the magnate observes. "Unseasonably dry and warm for April. The locals call it earthquake weather." He smirks. "Tell me, Professor, did the Palace Hotel meet your expectations?"

"First class."

"And *your* home is truly spectacular," Daniel adds.

Jan smiles. "I call it the Hippodrome." He draws our attention to a brightly colored brown and blue fresco on the wall opposite the bookshelf. It depicts Poseidon in a chariot drawn by a brace of horses; upon closer examination, the horses are mythological creatures, half horse and half fish. Jan anticipates my next question. “That creature is a hippocampus, and Poseidon is the Greek god of the sea, as well as seafarers, horses, and earthquakes. Appropriate, considering I’m in shipping.”

“I thought the Hippocampus is a region of the brain in charge of memory and navigation.”

“You are correct, Professor Angle. That part of the brain is shaped like a sea horse, hence its name.”

“And your name means ‘horses’ in Greek,” I continue, “hence, the Hippodrome.”

Daniel nods vigorously. “The Hippodrome reminds me of a castle I saw in Prague-” he begins.

“- The castle of Rudolf II?” the magnate suggests, rubbing his hands together. Clearly, he is pleased with the comparison.

“Well, yes,” Daniel continues. “Your mansion- the Hippodrome- has a kind of nobility.

Jan waves off the flattery, but a hint of a smile shows he likes it better than he lets on. "Nobility? I suppose. Some say this neighborhood is called Nob Hill because 'nob' is short for 'nobility.' He chuckles to himself. "Of course, others call it Snob Hill. Easy to see why. All those jumped up railroad tycoons built their mansions here after me."

The maid brings tea for three on a silver serving tray, along with a ripe pomegranate. The magnate addresses her. "Thank you, Sophia. Would you gentlemen like a cup of Earl Gray?"

We assent, and the young woman pours for each of us. She is short and slight, with curly brown hair and blue eyes, which her green dress and olive-green apron complement rather nicely. Her proportionally long arms and legs give her bearing an aspect of grace.

"Pomegranate?" she asks.

Jan dismisses her offer. "My favorite! But it is too early, and the gentlemen will be leaving soon."

"Beautiful china," I observe.

"Argentine," Jan says. "From Patagonia. Notice the silver inlay?" I feign interest.

Daniel turns his attention to the maid and favors her with a big smile. "Sophia- that is a nice name." Daniel is a good-looking young man, and he knows it. He is short and stocky, with broad shoulders, a barrel chest, thin blond hair, and startling blue eyes.

"Thank you." She responds with a crooked smile.

"It means 'wisdom' in Greek," he adds.

"If you say so, sir." She rolls her eyes, but resists saying what we are all thinking: how much wisdom does it take to pour a cup of tea?

The magnate dismisses her with a wave of the hand. "Cheeky girl."

"Good help is hard to find," I observe.

Jan grimaces. "Yes, well, the previous girl left on short notice. Said she couldn't sleep. Too many bad dreams." He rubs his hands together and nods to himself. "Will you be stopping on the way back to the University?"

"No," I answer, "we will take the English text directly to Miskatonic."

"My alma mater. Say 'hello' to Chancellor for me. We know each other personally." He waggles his eyebrows. "Tell him this is my gift in lieu of an annual donation." We both laugh. Jan Hippos is the school's most generous donor. He has already promised to underwrite an expedition to the far north, and the Hippos Foundation has established Miskatonic University's reputation as a world class institution for exploring the southernmost regions in the world, including Antarctica. "Is your copy back at the hotel?" he asks.

"Yes, at the hotel," I answer.

"You are certain the Latin translation in Buenos Aires was suppressed in 1890?"

"Yes," we answer at the same time. This is ground Daniel and I have covered before with the shipping magnate. Jan wants reassurance his Latin copy is the only existing one.

"The Argentine military burned it," I add. "Same goes for the French one. A secret society of priests burned it that same year."

"And the British Museum text went missing at the same time," Daniel chimes in.

The magnate gives a self-satisfied smile. "The British copy and mine have a lot in common."

In other words, I say to myself, *you stole it*, but I keep a carefully neutral expression.

"Now it is the centerpiece of my collection," he continues. "So! You will take your English translation to the Annex of the Occult?"

"Of course." I lift the reddish-orange and white nautilus shell from the table and examine it. The shell's pattern is fascinating, a Fibonacci spiral.

Jan Hippos suspects I am not really listening, and decides to drop a bombshell. "I am taking my English copy on a sea voyage."

"Is that wise?" I ask out of concern for his age, but Jan can only think of The Book.

"If anything happens, there will still be my Latin translation, and your English one back at Miskatonic."

Daniel strokes his chin. "Sir, may I inquire about your destination?"

Jan gives him a long stare. At first, I believe Jan will refuse to reveal it. He looks up at us and then down at the text on the coffee table several times before apparently reaching a decision to confide. "The destination is in the South Pacific, the geographic point farthest from land." He closes his eyes and recites the coordinate: "48°52'S, 123°23'W. Sir Francis Drake and Doctor John Dee mention it. Dee even connected it with Atlantis."

Atlantis again. Inwardly, I sigh. What is it about Atlantis? My professional expertise covers ancient languages, rare texts, and strange inscriptions, and Atlantis has no foundation in fact, other than mentions by Plato. And yet, the story brings out an eager and gullible willingness to buy into far-fetched myths, to chuck rationality in pursuit of preposterous, half-cocked, ill-formed conspiracy theories; why, I have even heard of scientists seeking the lost city! And now Jan Hippos, one of the richest men in the world, wants to go on an expedition to a theoretical point in the middle of the ocean? It is tempting to scoff, but I am sitting in his study, and he is a very wealthy supporter of the university. In our past conversations he has called San Francisco the Atlantis of the West, which is absurd. Despite my skepticism, or perhaps out of respect for his wealth, I hold my tongue.

"Will you continue to Kadath?" Daniel asks.

An awkward silence follows. At last, Jan speaks. "What do you know of it?"

"It would be better not to talk of this," I warn, "especially in a room with two copies of The Book."

Daniel is oblivious. "I have always been interested in Antarctica, sir, ever since I read Poe. And I have read the *Necronomicon*."

"Have you now?" Jan raises an eyebrow. Few people can read it and maintain their equilibrium. Perhaps Daniel is trying to impress the magnate. "In that case," Jan continues, "let me read you a passage. Tell me what you think." Before I can stop him, Jan opens it to the title page. "You'll have to forgive me; my Latin is a little rusty."

"Wait-" I exclaim.

"-Here we go," and he intones:

Flectere si nequeo superos, Acheronta movebo

"That's the dedication," Daniel asserts. "A quote from Virgil."

I raise a hand. "Freud used that as his dedication for *The Interpretation of Dreams*. Listen, reading this aloud is dangerous. Stop right now."

Jan waves his hand dismissively. "Yes, yes, Freud is all the rage these days. Now, where was I? He continues reading:

Manes abiit et sola videtur in locis frigidis

Several strange things happen simultaneously:

A small, rolling wave passes through the floor. There is a mirror on the wall behind Jan Hippos, and the wave ripples the surface of the mirror, too, distorting reflection and reality.

I feel like I have slipped out of time, but it is worse than that; I feel like my head is being turned inside out.

Loud thumps hit the window like large bugs banging against the glass, and the sound of buzzing insects fills my ears. It is still dark, so I cannot tell what is making the noise.

The brass horse, teacups, nautilus shell, and other loose knick-knacks rattle and bounce. The lights flicker and go out, leaving the study in pre-dawn darkness; almost immediately, the power comes back on.

"Whew!" Jan laughs. "Another earthquake. That one was stronger than most." He abruptly calls Sophia, fusses over the statue, teacups, and The Book, and calls her again.

"I hope we don't lose power," Daniel says.

"That would be inconvenient," the magnate says. "The sun won't come up for another hour. The electricity should be fine, but let me light a candle, just in case." He reaches for a brass candlestick on a nearby bookshelf and places it on the coffee table, next to The Book.

He then strikes a match and touches the small orange-yellow flame to the wick. Whether the lit candle was improperly seated in its hole, or accidentally knocked over by Hippos' palsied hand, I will never know, but it tips over and lands on The Book. A small wisp of gray smoke rises as one corner catches fire, and then, the monstrously big earthquake hits.

Everything jumps and bounces. The teacups go flying. China breaks on the tile floor. The nautilus shell rattles off the table and breaks into shards, and the brass horse statue clatters onto the floor. Cracks race across the ceiling and clouds of dust fill the study. The window shatters. The grandfather clock in the corner rocks, twists, and falls on the floor with a heavy boom. Its face reads 5:12. From somewhere down the hall, Sophia screams. Daniel and I are thrown from our chairs, and find ourselves on hands and knees, too shocked to act.

The mirror behind the magnate also shatters and its shards pepper his back. His eyes fix in an expression of surprise, and he slumps to the floor, face down. The back of his head is covered in blood.

An enormous rolling wave topples the heavy bookshelf, and it comes down on the helpless magnate's body, completely covering him and crushing him under its immense weight. It also extinguishes the candle and the fire consuming The Book. Blood flows from beneath the bookshelf in an expanding pool, to be almost immediately covered by dust and white masonry.

I panic. "We have to get out of here!" It is nearly impossible to stay on my feet. I crawl towards the door. Daniel trips over me.

We are frantic to escape the study, but Sophia stands in the doorway, barring our way. "Help him!" she demands, pointing at the fallen bookshelf. She shoves past and tries to move it herself. "Give me a hand, you lackwits!" Daniel and I attempt to lift it, but the bookshelf is much too heavy.

The mansion loses power and we find ourselves in darkness.

It is a terrifying and disorienting moment, being plunged into darkness while the ground shifts beneath us. Fortunately, Sophia takes command. "Follow me." She takes my hand. I grab Daniel, and together we leave the dark study and stumble into the hall. I carom down the dark hallway, pushing off one wall and then the other to keep my balance. Daniel follows. Sophia leads, navigating the way to the Hippodrome's front door, and we escape the building moments before another bout of buckling and heaving causes the mansion to fall in upon itself.

A granite wall surrounds the grounds. It has fallen. The main entry used to be through a wrought iron gate. That lays flat on the ground. There is no sign of the horse and buggy that brought us here. After a minute or so, the rolling and shaking finally stops. We walk onto one of the main thoroughfares in this neighborhood, Sacramento Street, and our position high on Nob Hill gives us an extraordinary view of the quake's devastation.

Throughout the city, unreinforced brick buildings have collapsed. The palatial residences of Huntington, Stanford, Hopkins, and Crocker lay in ruins. Water gushes from broken water mains, and gas lines break. The fires have already started. To the east, Chinatown is burning. To the southwest, the Castro District is on fire. Along California Street, wooden Victorian houses go up in flames. The tragic losses extend to the scientific libraries, including one of my favorites, the California Academy of Science on Market Street.

Behind us, the Hippodrome explodes in flame, fed by multiple gas leaks from the kitchen.

Daniel puts his hands on his knees and leans over to catch his breath. "What about the *Necronomicon*?" he finally asks.

I shake my head. "Both copies were in the Hippodrome. They burned."

"Bollocks!" Sophia declares. "How dare you gentlemen talk about a book! Everything I own is in that house, and now it's gone. All I have are the clothes on my back. Jan is dead, I don't have a job, I have no money, and I don't have anywhere to go."

I take her hand and apologize. "You are right. I was not thinking clearly. Please, come with us."

"There will be looting," Daniel says. "We'll protect you."

She grimaces. "I'll probably be safer with the looters." After giving both of us a hard look, she relents. "Beggars can't be choosers. Where are we going?"

"The Palace Hotel." The last existing copy of the *Necronomicon* is in my suite and that is my ulterior motive for going there, but I am not about to mention that in front of Sophia right now.

Sophia's voice shakes. "I don't have any money for a ticket."

I jingle three silver coins which I have in my pocket. It is all I have on me.

Daniel steps in. He reaches into his vest and produces the wad of money Jan Hippos paid us. "You saved our lives back there. We would not have escaped the Hippodrome if it were not for you. Don't worry about money. We've got you covered."

"Speaking of covering," I say, "Sophia, you are shivering. Take my jacket." Since she is wearing a dark green and olive green servant's outfit meant for indoors, she gratefully accepts my long black sack coat.

The three of us go down Sacramento Street and cut through a Lascar neighborhood to California Street. The Lascars- a people from the territories east of the Cape of Good Hope- have already fled.

Chinatown is on the north side of the street, and the damage there is appalling. Later I find out thousands of Chinese died, but they were dismissed as worthless opium fiends and worse, so no one bothered to count. We continue to Montgomery Street. It is only a little over a mile from Nob Hill to the Palace Hotel, but the rubble and cracks in the street slow progress. Water from broken mains flows down many of the cracks. Perhaps the most shocking sight of all is the sheer number of horses killed by falling bricks.

On Montgomery Street, a cast iron manhole cover blows into the air right in front of us, immediately followed by a water geyser. Its mist envelops us. That is remarkable enough, but what it even more remarkable is that the mist is so *cold.* At the geyser's peak, the droplets dissipate into a cloud of ice crystals that floats upward into the smoky twilight sky.

Sophia, Daniel, and I arrive at the Palace Hotel on the corner of California and Market Street shortly before sunrise. The red, white, and blue American flag with its 45 stars flies over the hotel, but like most stone and brick buildings, it has suffered earthquake damage. One corner has completely collapsed. My room, 901, is on the less damaged side. Sophia and Daniel wait while I circle the ruined carriage entrance where 70 foot Doric columns have fallen and now block the way. The entrance opens to a vast exposed interior space, an ornate lounge known as the Palm Court. It is in ruins. The skylight, a dome made from amber glass that once spanned the ceiling 120 feet above the floor, has shattered. Jagged glass shards cover the marble floor, along with masonry and other debris. The decorative tropical foliage is covered in white plaster dust, including the palm trees that made the Palm Court so famous. Chairs and tables have been tumbled every which way. A fresco depicting Persephone eating a pomegranate used to cover an entire wall. Cracks destroyed it. The same has happened to a fresco of a large stag on the opposite wall. While staying here, I used to greet the earnest young man sitting at the reception desk every morning. He would adjust his wire rim glasses and we would exchange pleasantries. Now he sits behind the desk motionless. His brown and yellow sweater is covered by plaster dust, and his glasses are coated too, but otherwise he appears unhurt. I approach him and call his name. When he fails to respond I check his pulse. He does not react when I touch his neck, but nevertheless, I detect a heartbeat. He is alive, but catatonic. There is nothing I can do for him, so I check the nearby elevators. The power is out, so of course the redwood paneled elevators no longer work. I take the stairs to my suite.

The room is in shambles. There is an electric call button for summoning staff, but I have not seen anyone since entering, and besides, the electricity is out. In the suite's parlor, a window looks over the city and street far below. While translating the *Necronomicon* into English I used to spend breaks staring out that window at the magnificent vista. Now it is broken, and I smell smoke from the burning city. The rising sun reveals an apocalyptic scene: billowing clouds of noxious smoke obscure the sky and much of the view, especially around Nob Hill and some of the Victorian houses on California Street.

The suite sways as an aftershock kicks up a cloud of dust. It is too dangerous to stay and pack, never mind take along my trunk. The English copy of the *Necronomicon*, the last existing copy, rests on the nightstand by my bed. I throw it in a small canvas satchel and exit as quickly as possible. On my way out I go to the reception desk and drag the catatonic clerk outside. With the help of Daniel and Sophia, I prop him against a wall on the opposite side of the street from the Hotel, at the intersection of Montgomery and Market. The street is in utter chaos. People wander through the rubble and step around the corpses of humans and dead horses. It is truly horrific.

"Let's get out of here," Daniel says.

Sophie surveys the streets. "Which way to the train station?"

Daniel points to the cable car line. It runs along Market Street, the city's main artery, but now it is out of commission. The rails have been deformed by the quake, and nearby, a derailed cable car lays on its side. "Maybe we should rethink traveling by train," he says.

Sophia and I agree.

"We could walk to the ferry," I suggest. "It is a straight shot down Market Street from here to the Union Ferry Depot. We can catch a train in Oakland."

"Are you sure this is the way to the ferry?" Sophia asks.

Billowing ochre smoke conceals lower Market Street. "Yes," I answer, "Normally the clock tower on the Ferry Building is visible from here."

"I doubt it is still standing," Daniel observes. "Do you think the ferry is running?"

"Sure," I reply with more certainty than I feel. The ferry terminal is one of the busiest transportation centers in the world, and I tell myself that even if the building is damaged, the ferries will still run.

Sophie purses her lips. "What if there's a tidal wave?"

"If there was going to be a tsunami, it would have happened by now."

That may or may not be true. I have no idea. Sophia accepts it, but Daniel gives me a disbelieving look. He has been around me long enough to know I specialize in ancient languages and rare texts, not tsunamis.

Daniel and I walk on either side of Sophia down Market Street. Although the wide thoroughfare is full of confused people- some injured, some in shock, others suddenly confronted with homelessness- the three of us do not fear for our safety. The police are out in force.

It turns out the local army fort, the Presidio, has reacted quickly and sent wagons of dynamite to police departments around the city. In theory, the police will create fire breaks by blowing up damaged buildings, and so restrict the out-of-control fires which already rage on Nob Hill, in Chinatown, and along California Street. Unfortunately, for all their good intentions, the police are not firemen and have no training in the use of explosives. From what I can see, they are making it worse. One detonation on California Street goes off too close to a gas main, resulting in an inferno. It is not going well for the firemen, either. They are powerless. It turns out all the city's aqueducts ran across the fault and every one ruptured in the quake. With hundreds of broken water mains and no water pressure, it is only a matter of time before the flames reach the Palace Hotel.

A crowd has gathered along an unusually large crack in the middle of the street. Policemen gather, and once organized, they direct the onlookers to step back. A local captain, a short, stocky, older man with a crew cut and blue eyes, is in charge. Daniel approaches the crack and looks over the edge. "It's deep," he observes.

"Get away from there," the captain barks. Police are shooting looters, so no one is about to argue. Daniel steps back, along with the rest of the crowd.

"Captain DeVert," a subordinate calls, "we're ready."

"Ready for what?" I ask the Captain.

"Ready to close that f****** crevasse. It's making people mad." That is quite a statement considering the surrounding mayhem- the looting, the fires, burst water mains, and the rubble in the streets- yet he is right. Something about that crevasse is terribly threatening. He glances at my satchel. "Stay out of the way," he sneers. "Don't make things worse."

DeVert gives the signal to detonate and the concussion from the dynamite blast nearly knocks me over. Coughing and waving in a cloud of dust and smoke, I bump into Daniel, who is still with Sophia. When the air clears, we realize Captain DeVert has done it. The dynamite works. The fissure has fallen in upon itself and closed, and despite the tragedy and ruin wrought by the quake, a sense of relief is almost palpable.

The three of us proceed down Market Street. Damage grows worse as we walk down the shallow slope towards the water, with leveled houses and office buildings flanking both sides. At last we reach the waterfront. Much to our surprise, the Ferry Building still stands, and so does the distinctive clock tower. The ferries and tugs are already coming to the rescue of the city and its survivors, thanks in part to the heroic and decisive actions of an intrepid young man from the Antipodes, Captain Marsh. We wait in a long line to board the first ship available, a sidewheel passenger ferry, the *Western Empire*. A surly Lascar mate with an unkempt beard and dirty greasy clothes collects the fare for the passage. He refuses to take the Indian Head pennies offered by Daniel; for payment, he will only accept the three silver coins from my pocket. With the satchel containing the English translation of the *Necronomicon* still in my hand, we ascend the walkway and begin the long journey back to Miskatonic University and the Annex of the Occult.

From the notes of Professor George Angle

The Greek Text

Evidence for the existence of a Greek translation of the *Necronomicon* is sparse.

1) 'Necronomicon' sounds Greek, but there is no such word in the Greek language. It was first composed in Arabic at the Palace of Wisdom, in Baghdad, and called *Al Azif*. In the mid-to-late 10th century Baghdad and Constantinople were in close contact and regularly exchanged ideas and texts, so it is possible an Arab text was sent there and translated into the archaic version of Greek spoken in the Byzantine Empire.
2) References to Greek mythology permeate The Book, including Scylla and Charybdis from the *Odyssey*, a whirlpool, and the rivers of Hell: Acheron, Lethe, Styx, Cocytus, and Phlegethon.
3) Other references include Persephone; her fruit and the color pomegranate; the name 'Kore,'

another name for the same goddess; and the connection of Persephone, the Queen of the Underworld, with myriad references to the subterranean.

In 1233 Pope Gregory IX started the Papal Inquisition to persecute heresy. He formally banned

the *Necronomicon* and specifically banned both Latin and Greek versions. It appears that if a Greek translation was ever made, it was destroyed at that time.

Point NEMO

Spring 1931

"Commander?"

"Yes, Penny?"

"Here- our latest position." Li Mei Penny, the Navigation and Communications Officer, sets down her heavy black sextant behind her swivel chair, and hands me a yellow slip of paper with the latest fix for the *Hippocampus*: "47°52'S, 123°23'W," she announces. "Point NEMO is sixty nautical miles due south."

She resumes her station on the far left of the bridge.

Our eventual destination is the Antarctic coast, but our real goal is Point NEMO, the Southern Pacific Uninhabited Area. It is the oceanic point of inaccessibility, the point farther from land than anywhere else in the world, with the nearest being an obscure island off Antarctica. The name NEMO originated with Jules Verne, the author of the science fiction classic *Mysterious Island*. In his book, the submarine *Nautilus* was commanded by Captain Nemo, which means 'no one' in Latin.

For us, NEMO means the middle of nowhere.

Captain Marshall, my co-captain, sits to my immediate right. He takes the yellow slip and dutifully records our position in the ship's log. Marshall is a handsome, middle-aged man, tall and deeply tanned, with dark hair and eyebrows and a deep devotion to his wife and children back in Auckland, New Zealand. He is the only crew member not directly associated with Miskatonic University. Marshall and I met in the Great War, the War to End All Wars. He brings a wealth of knowledge and experience to the mission, and we count ourselves fortunate that he agreed to join us aboard the *Hippocampus*.

Normally, the chair to his right would be occupied by a man of science, Frank H. Peabody. A deceased Greek magnate, Jan Hippos, originally funded this expedition through a foundation, and while he provided the money, Peabody provided the brains. The *Hippocampus* is his baby, a testament to his many innovations. Later this year, Peabody will lead an expedition to the Antarctic interior to test his latest invention, the revolutionary Peabody Drill. Peabody is a strong and rugged man with a bushy brown beard. Currently his leather swivel chair is empty; Miskatonic University's most famous engineer monitors the weapons station directly below the bridge.

Dr. Henry Armitage, Chief Librarian for Miskatonic University, sits in the jump seat behind us. Armitage is a hale 76 year old and his white beard is even longer than Peabody's beard. He likes to talk, especially when he is excited or nervous, and he has little use for engineers or the military. That is hardly surprising, since Armitage is an academic, mystic, and author of the famous treatise *Notes toward a Bibliography of World Occultism, Mysticism, and Magic* (Miskatonic University Press, 1927). He is also a renowned expert on literature relating to Atlantis.

Armitage is not the only academic on board. Dr Li Mei Penny has her doctorate in non-Euclidean geometry, and she is the youngest full professor on staff. She is the only female, the only person of Chinese descent, and except for me, the only one onboard who has never been married. She has a sturdy build, wears practical glasses with thick black frames, a dark plum jumpsuit, and she keeps her shiny black hair cut above the shoulder.

Unlike Armitage and Penny, my background is more practical. During the Great War I commanded a submarine. Since the advent of Pax Americana I have specialized in maritime archaeology. It seems unlikely Point NEMO will have anything to offer in terms of underwater research; nevertheless, we are drawing closer, and the atmosphere grows more electric.

"Penny," Marshall asks, "how does our celestial fix compare with dead reckoning?"

"Close. Avoiding the storms forced us to approach from the north. Our current course takes us due south to NEMO, but it will not be simple."

"Why not?"

"The currents are strange. They keep changing."

"Explain."

"The South Pacific circulates in a gigantic gyre bordered by Chile and Argentina's Tierra del Fuego, the land of fire; by the bare hills of Easter Island; and by the cold desert of Antarctica. It forms a gigantic swirling vortex centered on Point NEMO. It is like a giant whirlpool, and we are nearing the center. It should be calm, right?"

"Like the Sargasso Sea?" Armitage asks.

"Exactly. It should be calm in the center of the gyre, right? And yet, the closer we come to NEMO, the stronger the current around the vortex. And that's not all," she continues, "those storms should have created a lot of large swells, but the sea is nearly calm."

"Calm and clear and incredibly blue," Armitage chirps. He is remarkably resilient for his age, but he suffers from *mal de mer*, so calm seas make him happy.

"The water is clear," Penny says, "because there is no life in this ocean- no plankton, no fish, no sharks, no jellyfish, and no starfish. It is essentially a desert."

Armitage snorts. "I doubt that."

Armitage is sitting behind us, so it is easy for Penny to ignore him.

"There's more, Commander. If the instruments can be believed, the water temperature here is well below freezing."

"How can that be?" Marshall exclaims. He is proud of the *Hippocampus* and with good reason. The craft is state-of-the-art technology, from the engines to the sleek white hydrodynamic hull, to the sonar and radar, as well as weaponry, and Marshall advised Peabody on the design.

"Also," Penny adds, "the ship's chronometer is unreliable."

Marshall leans over and taps the glass faces of the temperature gauge and ship's clock, and then runs his finger around the brass settings. It has no effect, so 'for luck' he taps on a decal he placed on the dashboard, the New Zealand flag. The red, white and blue decal has a Union Jack in the upper left corner and four stars in the field representing the constellation of the Southern Cross. "Maybe it's a routine malfunction," he guesses. Penny and I exchange a glance. No expense was spared in the design and construction of the ship, thanks to the enormous endowment left by Jan Hippos. We both know there is no way that chronometer should malfunction.

Marshall furrows his brows and addresses Penny. "How do you know the problem is with the ship's time piece?"

She smirks. "I checked it against two watches I use for celestial navigation. There is no question. The chronometer is wrong."

Marshall hazards another guess. "Could it be a magnetic anomaly."

She shakes her head. "There may be some kind of anomaly, but magnetism would not affect the ship's clock."

Behind me, Armitage clears his throat. "According to accounts from Sir Francis Drake and Doctor John Dee, proximity to Atlantis caused anomalies." While I do not believe in the Atlantis myth, I have read the accounts of Drake and Dee, and Dr. Armitage is right: they do mention anomalies near point NEMO.

We press on in silence for quite some time, accompanied by the quiet hum of the *Hippocampus* engines as it slices through the flat, gun-metal gray ocean. The world outside has been reduced to basics. There are no Greek elements of fire and earth, only air and blue water. The fifth element, the ether, is also missing. Without it, the air and water appear empty and desolate.

Armitage cannot stand the quiet any longer, and breaks the silence with a quote:

Oed und leer das Meer

"What does that mean?" I ask.

"Empty and desolate the sea," he replies. "From *Tristan and Isolde*. A hero waits for his love to return from across the ocean, but there is no sail in sight."

Penny cannot resist. "So, for that lover, the ocean is a desert, right?"

Armitage ignores her. "For that lover, the ocean lacks its quintessence."

It is as if he has been reading my mind; both Armitage and I see the world outside the windows of the *Hippocampus* as lacking its quintessence, but I refuse to let pessimism win the day. "Perhaps we should include ourselves as an essential part of it, Dr. Armitage; perhaps the quintessence is spirit, or soul, or love."

Armitage chuckles. "Ever read any Freud?"

"A little. Didn't he write about love as an oceanic feeling?"

"Yes," he laughs. "Obviously Freud never visited Point NEMO."

Marshall and Penny stare straight ahead. They know Armitage. They know he wants to talk about Freud, and neither of them want to be drawn into one of his bookish debates.

When no one responds, Armitage continues anyway. "Professor Angle and I discussed Freud at length."

"I'm sure you did." My laconic reply does not deter him. Although my swivel chair allows me to turn around and face him, I do not. Armitage speaks from behind me, like the voice of a good or bad angel perched on my shoulder.

"Freud believes the conscious mind is like an island surrounded by the oceanic unconsciousness, just as the mythological river Acheron surrounds hell. Indeed, the dedication for the *Interpretation of Dreams* describes it with a quote from Virgil:

Flectere si nequeo superos, Acheronta movebo.

"Meaning?"

"If I cannot bend the heavens above, I will cross the Acheron," he answers. "You see, Freud fears the subconscious- that is, the world of dreams- will rise and overflow its banks, drowning the conscious mind in dreams. As a specialist in maritime archaeology, Commander, I am sure you can appreciate that point of view."

He pauses and waits expectantly for my reply.

"So... hell is the same as the subconscious mind?"

"Harrumph. You misunderstand me, sir."

"All right, then. Is the subconscious the source of the oceanic feeling of love? Or is the oceanic feeling something threatening to the conscious mind, since it involves the loss of the self's boundaries for the sake of union with the beloved?"

"That is what exploration is all about," Armitage declares, "whether it is maritime archaeology or the interpretation of dreams. The point is this: exploration expands borders; discovery reveals truth. Remember what Socrates said: "the unexamined life is not worth living."

How did that work out for Socrates? I wonder, but that is better left unsaid.

Armitage continues. "It is nobler to question and explore and discover and interpret, even if the answer is dark, than to meekly accept; in other words, as Milton said, 'it is better to reign in Hell than serve in Heaven.' We fulfill our highest calling when we plumb the depths."

I turn in my chair to face him. "Instead of the subconscious overflowing its banks and flooding the conscious, wouldn't it make more sense to compare the subconscious with a whirlpool violently drawing the surface world down into its vortex?"

"Eh?" Armitage scoffs. "It figures you would think that way. Always the military man. Always assessing a threat. Now, if Atlantis represents the subconscious mind-" he begins.

"-Oh, for heaven's sake," the voice of Peabody crackles over the intercom. Apparently, he has been listening from his station below, and the engineer has little patience for this kind of talk.

"Cloud bank moving in," Marshall announces. I swivel in my chair and face the windshield. From the south, dark towering clouds loom above the horizon. They roil and roll towards us like a thousand charging black horses.

"Is that a squall?" Armitage asks nervously.

Penny purses her lips. "Those clouds will interfere with my celestial observations. Well, we are close enough to navigate from here with just dead reckoning, right?" She addresses Armitage. "Professor, I've been thinking-"

"Beginners luck," Peabody jokes over the intercom. "Quick, Penny, before the thought dies of loneliness."

She rolls her eyes. "There's a reason we keep you downstairs and by yourself, Peabody."

Marshall reaches for a switch on the dash. "Don't make me turn off the intercom."

Penny laughs and addresses Armitage. "Tell me, Professor, what about ghosts? Are they psychological projections?"

"Ghosts are dreams," he answers. "Dreams are ghosts. Dreams haunt our consciousness. So do nightmares. This is certainly true of the ghosts from the *Necronomicon*.

"I doubt it," I state, keeping an eye on the approaching squall. "You're not the only one who has spoken with Professor Angle."

"I know his opinions on the matter," Armitage primly says.

"So do I. According to him, the ghosts of the *Necronomicon* are not psychological projections. They are not specters from history. They have nothing to do with a concept of afterlife, or heaven, or hell. The ghosts are real, and they are a blank to us. They are violent and utterly uncaring, a malignant emptiness unconnected to humanity."

"They inspire dreams," Armitage insists.

"Not for me."

"Me neither," Marshall adds.

"Harrumph. Artistic natures are more susceptible."

"Well, no need to worry about the *Necronomicon*," Penny says. "The only copy is in the Miskatonic Library Annex of the Occult under lock and key, right?"

"Correct," Armitage responds. "While I am away, the Assistant Librarian, Arthur Dyer, is in charge of the Annex."

"What about the Old Ones?" I ask him. "Where do they fit in? Do they even exist?"

"Atlantis is their city," he replies.

"Maybe," Penny says, "the cold ghosts of the *Necronomicon* are the spirits of the Old Ones in a different phase. Maybe they inhabit another time, or space, or dimension, and distort this one."

"Maybe," Armitage says, stroking his white beard, "but we will never know. Professor Angle and I often disagree; however, we do agree about the talisman. The idol is a physical representation of an Old One, and it moves from north to south-"

"- From the arctic to the Antarctic."

"Correct, Commander. It moves through the agency of humans. Of course, compared with the Old Ones, humans are weak and undependable, and the talisman destroys human reasoning and judgment as the idol makes its way south, while stoking rage."

"Wait." Penny says. "Is it a talisman or an idol?"

"Professor Angle and I argued about this." He waits to see what I will say, but I hold my piece. "Idol or talisman? It could be both. An idol is an object for worship. A talisman is magical. Based on what we know, when used for an initiation, the talisman alters consciousness. It inspires devotion to The Book, and rage against the uninitiated; in other words, the talisman inspires attacks against those with an incompatible consciousness. Professor Angle believes the initiates seek to bring the Old Ones back to physical form."

"Poppycock," Peabody exclaims over the intercom.

Armitage can barely conceal his irritation. "Peabody, like most engineers, you lack imagination."

Peabody responds with a rude and rather imaginative suggestion. We grip our armrests as the ship plows into a bigger swell.

"The sea is becoming choppier," Marshall observes. He is right, of course. The successive waves feel like hoof beats kicking the bow. Inside the *Hippocampus* it is growing colder.

The motion makes Armitage nervous, and he tends to ramble when on edge. "What is imagination," he intones, "but a waking dream? It starts when you open your eyes, and open a book, and read- the waking dream of imagination. It unlocks a previously unseen, unknown world. These dreams of imagination are different from the dreams of sleep, of course, for dreams of sleep are fleeting and unremembered. Like the ghosts of the *Necronomicon*, they haunt us- unseen, but hovering at the edge of perception. And yet, they all involve a kind of magic, don't you agree?"

"Mysticism, Dr. Armitage?" Marshall asks.

"The ghosts are so mystical; you can't even see them!" Peabody quips.

"Dreams and ghosts..." Penny muses. "Is all this an elaborate metaphor for death and an afterlife?"

"Have you ever seen a ghost?" Marshall asks Armitage. "The only ghost I've ever seen was in a play- Shakespeare's father in *Hamlet*."

Armitage shakes his head. "The ghosts of the *Necronomicon* are unlike Shakespearian ghosts. And they are not a metaphor. They have nothing to do with an afterlife, or some sort of inexplicable karmic revenge mechanism. The ghosts invoked by The Book are far more terrifying than those Shakespearian "dreams of sleep" about that "undiscovered country from which no traveler returns" because the dreams inspired by the *Necronomicon* do not involve "the dread of something after death," but something worse, far worse."

"What could be worse than that?" Marshall asks.

"A blankness, a violent negation utterly unconnected with human concerns, or even cause and effect." Armitage takes a deep breath. "On one hand, we have being and causality and sequential time; on the other hand, we face a cold emptiness outside time, an absolute zero, a negation without any connection to being and its cessation. Bottom line? There is no "undiscovered country." There never was. When confronted with the reality of The Book and the ghosts, we must conclude that there is no afterlife with a country waiting to be explored."

Peabody snorts. "Gawd, get a job."

"Marshall, what is that?" I ask. A large greenish-yellow blip has appeared at the edge of his radar screen's range, roughly 30 miles away. He furrows his brows. Penny leaves her station to lean over his shoulder. That blip is heading straight for the *Hippocampus*.

"Another ship," Marshall answers.

"Are you sure?" Peabody asks over the intercom.

"Of course it's a ship," I answer. "What else could it be?" I ask.

Marshall slowly shakes his head. "No one knows we're here."

"They do," Penny says. "But how?"

We are in the middle of nowhere. There is no chance another ship would be in this area, so far from ports and shipping lanes. That other ship is here for one reason. They are here for us. How did they know?

The *Hippocampus* was built at the Bath Iron Works in Maine. Funding was lavish, thanks to Jan Hippos. No expense was spared. Ah, the cost. The ship was longer than a luxury yacht but shorter than a German U-Boat; its size and its sleek, hydrodynamic design was bound to attract attention. The *Hippocampus* was built for research and luxury, but its weaponry would also draw attention. Finally, as it traveled south, the ship's conspicuous presence at the ports of Buenos Aires and Ushuaia would have been hard to miss. Incidentally, according to Professor Armitage and Professor George Angle, the Greek shipping magnate Jan Hippos embraced associations with his name. When most Americans hear 'Hippos' they think of a hippopotamus. 'Hippos' means 'horse' in Greek, so 'hippopotamus' means 'river horse.' 'Hippocampus' refers to a mythological beast-half horse, half fish, and dear to Poseidon; hence, the name of this ship. By the way, hippocampus also refers to a small region of the brain that is shaped like a sea horse. It oversees memory and navigation and, as it turns out, it is shaped like a sea horse. The British often depict hippocampi pulling a sea chariot guided by Britannia, a symbolic promotion of 'Rule Britannia/Britannia rule the waves.' Sometimes, the charioteer is a member of British royalty, and carries a trident and a shield with the Union Jack on it. In any case, Jan Hippos perished in the San Francisco Earthquake of 1906, leaving his Foundation to fund exploration of the southern seas, the Southern Continent, and the search for Atlantis.

As for that other ship, there are many ways they could have known about us, but the more important question is this: what do they intend to do?

Marshall times the radar return. "They are traveling at the same speed as us, 15 knots."

For its size, the *Hippocampus* is one of the fastest ships in the world, capable of going over 30 knots. For now, I choose not to reveal that capability. "Penny, hail them."

She calls on various frequencies. "No response, Commander. There is a lot of electromagnetic interference. Perhaps there is an electrical storm within the cloud bank. Just a second-"

"What is it?"

"I am picking up a call. Very faint. Putting it on speaker:

Mayday, Mayday. This is the Miskatonic flight bound for the Chthonic Dome...

Someone- a man- is declaring an emergency," she continues, "and it is a flight, so that must be an aircraft."

"The Chthonic Dome is in Antarctica," Armitage states. "There are no Miskatonic University planes there." Peabody agrees.

"So, the call does not come from the approaching ship," I conclude.

"No, Commander. Must be an echo off the ionosphere."

"Penny, extend the mast telescope as high as possible." The ocean horizon is 12 miles away. The telescope's extra altitude will give us a slight advantage in identifying the other craft sooner, while it is still over the horizon. She takes her place at the telescope.

Armitage nervously strokes his long beard. "I wonder how much they know about us?"

Peabody answers over the intercom. "Not nearly enough, I'll wager."

"Do you think they are hostile?" he asks.

"*I* do," the engineer answers from below. "Commander, weaponry and countermeasures are ready."

"Good work. Prepare the forward gun." The *Hippocampus* has a .20 Oerlikon autocannon mounted up front, a military marvel invented by men and women of science, with a high fire rate and high capacity magazines. The long, narrow gunmetal gray barrel can accurately hurl shells long distances; right now, the other vessel is out of range.

"Visual contact," Penny announces. "Looks like a small warship, a frigate or corvette. Here, Commander, take a look."

I take her place at the telescope and grip the handles. The rising storm is causing a lot of chop, and it is not easy to keep my balance. "Probably Great War vintage. That's good for us. Unless they have made modifications, we should be faster than them and better equipped." I go back to my chair, and Penny replaces me at the telescope.

"Current is growing stronger," Marshall says. Not only that, the water temperature has dropped even further, at least according to the temperature gauge, and the color of the ocean has transitioned from clear blue to gunmetal gray to an inky black. Meanwhile, the squall will soon envelop both ships.

"Oh!" Penny exclaims. "Puffs of smoke from their forward gun turret. They are firing at us."

"Evasive maneuvers." Marshall turns to port and accelerates. "Range?"

"Ten miles," he responds. Fountains of spray erupt in the ocean a mile or so off the bow.

That brings a smile to my face. "They don't know the range of their own weapons. That means they are either overaggressive, inexperienced, or incompetent. Peabody, fire the autocannon."

"But-"

"-We are also out of range. I know. It is just a demonstration. I want them to see the muzzle flash. Maybe it will force another mistake. Fire."

The enemy ship responds to the flash of the autocannon by turning to starboard. Their new course gives a profile. A single gun turret tracks us from a raised forecastle, and an unmanned anti-aircraft gun can be seen amidships. Aft, a depth charge rack is loaded with canisters.

"They're distracted. Good. Retract the autocannon and the telescope. Penny, have a seat. Marshall, deploy our external shell once we've slowed to within safety parameters."

While Marshall and I run a call-and-response checklist, the *Hippocampus* puts on a demonstration of technological wizardry. It deploys a shield which unfolds, extends, and encompasses the entire ship in a protective white shell. The process is incredibly *fast*. The shield, essentially a second airtight hull, slides across the windshield last, leaving only internal lighting on the bridge. Without a view, claustrophobia torments Armitage, and he moans.

"On instruments," Marshall calls. "Engineer, deployment complete. How does the seal look?"

"Testing and… good seal."

"Marshall, extend stabilizer fins fore and aft."

"Extended."

"Submerge." Swirling bubbles cascade past the hull's exterior. Soon, the world outside becomes nearly silent. The hull has two layers but no insulation, and now the cold penetrates the bridge and the rest of the ship.

"How deep can we go?" Armitage asks.

"Not as deep as a U-Boat," Marshall answers.

Now that we are underwater, the rough chop that made Armitage seasick has abated, but the old man seeks distraction from his claustrophobia.

"How deep is it at Point NEMO?"

"No one knows."

Armitage moans again. “Freud came out with a new book, *Civilization and its Discontents*, and I’m wondering-”

“-Not now, Professor,” I interrupt, and address Marshall. “Up periscope.”

“Periscope up.”

“Sonar?” I ask.

“Tracking.”

“All ahead full.” Marshall acknowledges. Not only is the *Hippocampus* a submarine, but it can travel twice as fast underwater as most surface vessels.

“Penny, calculate a course for optimum angle of attack for the torpedoes.”

“Done.” She gives Marshall the heading and he makes a small correction.

“Peabody, load and arm torpedoes one and two.” From the deck below the engineer monitors the process. An autoloader slides each 2,600 pound torpedo into its tube. Torpedoes one and two carry 500 pound TNT warheads, while three and four carry modified 1,000 pound warheads. The torpedo designs include revolutionary sonar tracking capabilities and proximity fuses, as well as options for timing detonations. His voice narrates the process: "tube one... loaded. Tube two... loaded."

"Arming torpedoes." I flip a red safety cover and flip one toggle, and then another. "Setting proximity fuses. One armed. Two armed."

Through the periscope, tiny figures are visible frantically running around the deck of the enemy vessel. Some go to the depth charge rack and drop several canisters. The depth charge detonations are much too far away to have any effect, and fortunately for us, the other ship lacks a depth charge launcher which could hurl them in our direction. One crewman aimlessly fires the anti-aircraft gun into the sea. The forward turret fires and misses us by a wide margin.

Penny is extremely angry. "What is wrong with them?"

"Perhaps they are under the influence of the talisman," Armitage says. "They act irrationally. They act like they are too enraged to think."

Armitage may have a point, but I do not care. Sinking the ship in these cold waters will certainly kill everyone on board, but they brought this upon themselves, and now, it is them or us. I like our chances. "Marshall, are we in firing range?"

"We're at the outer edge."

"Go closer," Penny demands. She is extremely agitated and can barely sit still in her seat.

"No need," I say. "Let the homing sonar and proximity fuses do their job."

She slaps her armrests. "I want to see the whites of their eyes!"

Marshall and I exchange glances. Penny is normally calm and unemotional.

Marshall leans towards her. "Are you all right?"

She hugs herself. "It's too cold." She is right about that. The low ocean temperature outside the double hull is making itself felt. The temperature gauge shows impossibly low readings.

The hash marks in the view from the periscope show optimal range.

"Fire one."

Marshall flips another red safety cover and depresses a white button.

"Torpedo away," Peabody announces over the intercom.

"Locked on. Running true." Marshall rubs his hands together. "Sure is cold."

"Turn to port," I command. "Penny, give him a heading for Point NEMO."

The ship sees the wake of the approaching torpedo and turns to evade. The torpedo tracks and closes. A direct hit! It impacts just below the waterline, beneath the forecastle. Apparently the detonation ignites the ammunition stored beneath the gun turret because the first explosion is followed by a much larger secondary one, a yellowish-orange fireball that obliterates the ship.

Penny pumps her fist and yells in triumph. No one bothers to ask if we should rescue survivors.

"Are we going to surface?" Armitage meekly asks. After years of commanding a submarine during the Great War, I am used to the conditions inside a submarine, but the old man is caught between a rock and a hard place: surfacing means rough seas and seasickness, while staying submerged means claustrophobia.

"No," I answer, "we will stay down here." The squall line drives larger and larger swells before it, and now the rain has overtaken us and there is nothing more to see on the surface. "Down periscope."

"The current is growing stronger," Marshall observes.

"No matter," I say, "we will be at Point NEMO soon. Maintain 30 knots."

Penny fidgets and taps a foot. She picks a pointless argument with Marshall over the temperature gauge, which continues to show impossibly cold water temperatures. He drums his fingers, taps the red, white, and blue New Zealand flag decal out of habit, and returns to drumming his fingers. The closer we approach to NEMO, the more agitated the crew becomes, including myself.

The current continues to strengthen, and Penny's review of the plotting data reveals it is growing stronger the closer we approach to NEMO. Even worse, the Hippocampus is listing to starboard. Loose objects slide across the deck- papers, pens, a protractor, and more.

Armitage cannot contain himself. "What is going on? Are we sinking?"

Penny pounds her arm rests with her fists. "Go back! It's too cold!"

The temperature gauge shows the outside water temperature is as cold as liquid nitrogen. Inside the craft, our exhalations create white plumes. Penny undoes her seat harness, lunges forward, and pounds the gauge, yelling in incoherent rage.

I attempt to subdue her by wrapping her in my arms. I am much stronger, but she is frantic, and with the deck listing at an angle it is hard to stay on my feet, never mind restraining her before she can damage the dash; fortunately, most of the dials and gauges are made from brass and steel and heavy glass, or protected by safety covers, so she is unable to do any harm. Marshall moves to undo his seat harness, but I wave him off. "Take the helm." I key the intercom. "Peabody, come up to the bridge. Now. Help me."

"On my way."

Peabody is a burly, energetic man- middle aged, average height, and exceptionally strong, with a full beard, sharp nose, and dark intelligent eyes. We are both bigger than Penny, but she fights so hard it takes both of us to strap her into her chair. The steep slope of the deck makes it even more difficult to restrain her. Marshall struggles to control the craft. Armitage grips his chair, closes his eyes tight, and groans. Much more of this strain will be too much for the old man.

"Marshall, emergency surface. Collapse the shell. Leave the fins extended."

He complies, and the *Hippocampus* quickly returns to the turbulent surface. As the shell retracts from the windshield it reveals a shocking sight. The ship lists because it is racing along the wall of an enormous funnel, a whirlpool miles wide and towering above us, and we are already halfway down the wall and being pulled towards the bottom. There it is below us: Point NEMO.

Inside the vortex it is twilight; high above, eerie shifting mists alternately reveal and conceal the far upper reaches. Stranger yet, fine droplets separate from the wall and fall upwards, towards the foamy rim and gray heavens. Nine concentric metallic rings form the watery walls, possibly internal supports for the infernal maelstrom. The upper three rings appear to be brass, the middle three tin, and the bottom rings glow with a bright reddish light from within- orichalcum.

In a strangled voice Armitage manages one word: "Atlantis." Penny thrashes in her seat and screams "too cold" over and over. The roar of the maelstrom makes it nearly impossible to concentrate, the bridge is freezing, and no one is dressed for it. The ship violently shimmies from side to side.

"We're losing control!" Marshall yells.

"Turn to port." I must shout just to make myself heard. "Head down. Build up speed."

Marshall understands, and turns the bow towards the depths of the whirlpool. The extra speed re-establishes control and maneuverability, but now we are heading towards whatever fate awaits us at the bottom.

Far below, through swirling mists, we catch glimpses of the bottom, a gigantic jumble of moss-encrusted rocks. This must be an undiscovered sea mount, a Mountain of Madness, centered within the focal point of the South Pacific gyre. It is an anti-island. Atop the chaotic rock pile stands a structure built from some sort of rotten greenish-black basalt. Although the very existence of the structure defies logic and physics, its form takes definition from columns- some standing, some leaning against one another, and others fallen over- and from piles of blocks tumbled against one another in geometrically impossible shapes. Just looking at them makes me feel like my head has been turned inside out. Penny might be able to make sense of this non-Euclidean nightmare, but she continues to throw herself against her restraints, and scream. It appears she has completely lost her mind.

And then, sitting atop the chaotic structure of Atlantis, the mists momentarily allow a clear view, and we discern the unworldly creature.

Armitage points, eyes round with horror. “An Old One!”

A modern Charybdis perches atop the temple of Point NEMO. This is no mythical monster from the *Odyssey*- the enormous creature is unquestionably real, and we instinctively know it is far older than any Greek myth. It combines elements of a starfish, black beetle, and cactus, with five thick arms and nodes surrounding its top. One menacing arm lifts and sways from side to side; rippling patterns run up and down the cilia of the arm in shades of indigo, neon blue, and reddish orange. The creature points at us and issues a roar that covers the entire aural spectrum. The ultra-low frequency thrums in our bones. The ultra-high envelops and twists the innermost parts of our minds.

Penny suffers a seizure and slumps against her restraints, motionless, a thin trickle of blood running from her nose and ears. Armitage goes catatonic. His eyes roll back into his head, his mouth hangs open, and his features go slack. Marshall loses consciousness.

The aural blast stops, and Peabody sees what has happened to Marshall. Peabody is badly shaken, and he has a mad gleam in his eye, but at least he can still function. "I've got this," he says. He unfastens Marshall's harness, roughly pulls the unconscious Co-Captain from the chair and onto the deck and takes his seat. The engineer quickly fastens his harness.

"Peabody, load and arm torpedoes three and four."

"Loaded and armed." The bridge is freezing, and each exhalation, each word, each syllable is accompanied by a white cloud.

"Target the building with three."

"Target acquired."

"Fire three."

"Torpedo away."

"Target the creature."

"Target acquired."

"Fire four."

"Torpedo away. Both locked on and running true."

Despite the strong currents, both torpedoes are on target, but as impossible as it seems, their path is neither straight, nor curving with the current.

"Turn us towards the funnel's top."

Peabody clenches his teeth with the effort. "Helm not responding. The current..."

The walls of the whirlpool are becoming even steeper. We have slipped past the middle rings, the ones made of tin, and into the region of the orichalcum rings. There is a risk of losing contact with the wall of churning water and falling to the bottom.

"Can we deploy the shell and submerge before the torpedoes explode?"

"Maybe."

"Do it."

The shell extends across the windows. In that last moment before it closes the sight of the Old One and its unholy temple burns itself into my mind. The first torpedo detonates in a yellowish orange bloom, obliterating the assemblage of rocks and fallen columns. The second one detonates, and the nightmarish creature issues its last and strongest aural blast as it disappears in a fireball. The orichalcum rings splinter into reddish metallic shards; the lower rings deconstruct, followed by the structural failures of the tin and brass rings. The whirlpool wall collapses and the turbulence is simply incredible. The *Hippocampus* rolls end over end, and Peabody struggles to regain control and turn against the current, upstream-

From the notes of Professor George Angle

Shortly after the Point NEMO expedition I interviewed the lone survivor, Engineer Frank H. Peabody. The rest of the crew- the Commander, the Co-Captain, Dr. Li Mei Penny, and Dr. Henry Armitage- perished. The *Hippocampus* was badly damaged. It is a testament to the ingenuity of the engineer that he kept it afloat long enough to reach a sea lane and call for rescue. The ship was scuttled. Peabody eventually reached Tierra del Fuego and returned by plane. According to Peabody, the whirlpool collapsed when the *Hippocampus* destroyed the temple and the creature. Afterwards, flecks of bright red orichalcum dotted the sea, but he could not retrieve any of the mythical metal. It is also worth noting that the sole survivor, Frank Peabody, is the only living person to ever see an Old One.

Unfortunately, to this day, Peabody remains deep in denial. He refuses to acknowledge the possibility that the structure atop the sea mount was Atlantis. He also refuses to acknowledge the nature of the Old One, insisting on non-sensical explanations about squids, humpback whales, and the like. He will not allow himself to be in the same room as the *Necronomicon*, never mind read from it, which is understandable. Daniel Forth and I delivered the last existing copy to the Miskatonic Library Annex of the Occult, and it is kept under lock and key, so Peabody should have no problem avoiding it.

Despite the harrowing experience at Point NEMO, Peabody vows to return to Antarctica by aeroplane as soon as practical, accompanied by the new Chief Librarian, Arthur Dyer, and various men and women of science. Peabody intends to test his latest invention, a revolutionary drill, in the Antarctic interior.

He insists on referring to Antarctica as 'Kadath.'

GHOSTS
from the
MOUNTAINS
of
MADNESS
901
DONALD McEWING

The Peabody Expedition 1931

"Danforth! This way!" I waved for him to follow me, and together we ran through the gloomy Antarctic twilight. The aeroplane was our only hope for escape, and it was not far off, but the high altitude of the plateau made the smallest exertion difficult, the incredibly cold temperatures threatened our lives, and our heavy winter furs slowed us even further.

The greatness of my fear made my head ache and my heart pound; gasping for breath, I clutched the think black leather-bound journal to my chest, and kept running. I had intended to save The Book as well, but it was too late for that now; it had been left behind with the members of the expedition, and there was nothing I could do about that, nothing but save Danforth and myself...

About the Author

Donald McEwing is married and lives in Tigard, Oregon with two cats. His background includes a classical education in English literature, German literature, Eastern religions, and philosophy at one of the nation's top universities, as well as an MBA. Careers include serving as a B-52 bombardier in SAC with the rank of Captain, providing financial services at a brokerage firm, teaching high school English and World History, and selling computer training for end users and people in IT.

Upstream provides the historical background for the next two novellas, *Ghosts from the Mountains of Madness* and *Against the Ghosts*. If all goes as planned, the three novellas will be published in one volume, *The Ghost Trilogy*, in 2020. These novellas and the first novel, *Nouveau Haitiah*, are already available as e-books and in hard copy.

Special thanks to illustrator Julia Thummel, and proofreader Gail Fisher for invaluable feedback.

Made in the USA
Monee, IL
28 May 2023